UNDERCOVER GEISHA

JUDITH CRANSWICK

www.judithcranswick.co.uk

Also by Judith Cranswick

The Aunt Jessica Mysteries
Murder in Morocco
Undercover Geisha

The Fiona Mason Mysteries
Blood on the Bulb Fields
Blood in the Wine
Blood and Chocolate
Blood Hits the Wall
Blood Across the Divide
Blood Flows South

Standalone Psychological Suspense
All in the Mind
Watcher in the Shadows
A Death too Far

Nonfiction
Fun Creative Writing Workshops for the New Writer

PROLOGUE

The silence in the empty building was broken by the creak of floorboards in the corridor.

Kenji Nakamura looked up; his pen poised over his notes. He'd always known that Water Dragon would send someone, but not this soon.

His mouth went dry. Every nerve in his body tensed. For a moment he could not move. He had two choices. Either brazen it out or switch off the small reading lamp and cower in the kneehole of his desk. Too late to hide now. The assassin already knew he was here alone in his office. The rest of the staff had left the building long ago. Only the night guard remained, though chances were that the man was now sprawled on the floor of his cubbyhole with his throat cut.

The screen door slid open and three black-clad figures entered.

'Can I help you, gentlemen?' Kenji was proud of the lack of tremor in his voice.

For a long moment they said nothing, then one stepped forward and growled, 'You have taken something that does not belong to you.'

'I'm sorry, I don't understand,' Kenji lied.

'Don't play games. Water Dragon wants his property back.'

One of the other men walked over to the large portrait of Kenji's grandfather who had founded the company after the war, building it up into one of Tokyo's most successful finance houses. The picture was moved aside to reveal the safe.

'Give him the number,' barked the spokesman at Kenji.

There was little point in attempting to hold out. '160184.'

Papers, legal documents and bundles of pristine banknotes still in their wrappers, were pushed aside.

The searcher turned and shook his head.

The spokesman drew a knife, its blade glinted in the poor light. 'Where is the notebook?'

'I don't have any notebook.'

At a signal from the spokesmen, his two bullyboys systematically pulled open every drawer in the filing cabinets emptying the contents onto the floor.

Kenji closed his eyes as the man slowly walked towards him brandishing the knife. He had known the risks, but enough was enough. Thanks to Water Dragon, he had become little more than a puppet in his own family business. Killing his son had been the final straw. Someone had to try to expose the extortion and corruption that threatened to pervade every level of Japanese hierarchy. He could only pray to the gods that his elaborate plan would work. There was no one else he could trust. Water Dragon had senior policemen, judges and politicians on his payroll.

As his head was pulled back, he looked up into the cold, black eyes of the man sent to kill him. He felt the edge of the blade resting across his throat.

'One last chance or you die.'

A slow smile spread across Kenji's lips as he said his final words. 'You're too late. Tell Water Dragon his reign is over. His empire is about to collapse and there is nothing he can do to stop it.'

CHAPTER 1

'Well young man, how much longer are you going to continue to take advantage of your Aunt Jessica? You can't expect to sponge on her indefinitely.'

I'll swear the old bat had waited until my mother was out of the room and could not spring to my defence. Aunt Maud glared at me with the same penetrating stare that had turned my knees to jelly since I had first learnt to walk.

'I-I've already started looking for somewhere else,' I stammered. 'While we were so busy getting everything ready for the trip to Japan, there really hasn't been much time. I've been helping her put her talks up on slides and sorting out a few technical problems she was having with her computer. Plus helping out with some of the research. Japanese history isn't her strongest area of expertise.'

'Then perhaps she should never have accepted the assignment.' Aunt Maud never wasted an opportunity to find some reason to criticise her sister. I was not the only one who failed to make the grade in the Hamilton family. Perhaps it was one of the reasons Aunt Jessica and I got on so well together. Though I have to admit, Aunt Maud's disapproval washed over Aunt Jessica like rain running off an umbrella. It bothered her not at all. It simply amused her, which probably irked her elder sister even more. Sadly, I did not possess the same skill. Aunt Maud's ability to make me feel inadequate has never lessened in all the thirty-odd years of my existence.

'Aunt Jessica did refuse at first, but they kept on at her. One of the tour company directors who she knows personally, pleaded with her and said the trip would have to be cancelled if she wouldn't step in.'

'I fail to see, Harry, what that has to do with you having to move in with your aunt. What possible help could you be? You know even less about Oriental cultures than she does.'

'Well, yes. But as I said, I can help with the technical side of things. All the Japanese hotels we'll be staying in have top-of-the-range facilities so I'm putting all her lectures into presentations on her laptop. That way, she'll be able to show pictures and we won't have to take so much in the way of handouts and so on.' I realised I was babbling, and Aunt Maud wouldn't understand what I was on about anyway. I doubt she'd ever seen a computer, let alone used one. My mother was the only one of the three sisters living in the Hamilton house who even owned a mobile phone and that was only because I'd bought it for her. I'm not sure she ever used it, but that was another issue altogether. 'There's been so much to do, it's been easier to help if I'm on the spot.'

'I was not only referring to you lodging with your aunt,' she interrupted my flow. 'I can appreciate you may have found a way of being occupied on her behalf in preparation for this tour, but what happens when you return home? You need to find yourself a job, young man. I presume you will be returning to Bedford?'

'Probably not,' I hedged. I had no intention of going back. Too many bad memories. Besides, I'd already handed in my notice on the dingy one-roomed flat three months ago when Aunt Jessica had first invited me to be her secretary-cum-dog's body just before our trip to Morocco. We kept up the pretence that it was more convenient for me to stay with her, but Aunt Jessica must have known that I was only days away from being homeless. My funds had dwindled to such a low ebb that I could no longer afford the rent on the pokey bedsit I'd been forced to move to after I'd had to sell my house following my dismissal from the bank.

On the pretext of having to finish off my packing, I escaped back up to the box room upstairs. My grip was already zipped up and ready on the floor in the middle of the room. I'd even put the dirty bedlinen in the wash basket, collapsed the camp bed and put the duvet and pillows back in the cupboard. There was still nearly an hour before the bus left the village centre for Norwich and I could escape.

I went over to the window, leant forward, elbows on the sill and looked out over the back garden to the flat featureless expanse of the Breckland fens. The grey leaden skies did nothing to lighten my mood. Even by Norfolk standards, considering we were well into March, there was little sign of Spring.

Aunt Maud might never miss an opportunity to express her disappointment in me, but I had to confess she did have a point. I could hardly expect Aunt Jessica to sub me indefinitely. Not counting four weeks in a packing warehouse on minimum wage, I'd been unemployed for almost a year before she'd offered me a temporary job, but she hardly needed me. True, because she spent most of her time researching for the next trip, I'd taken over the running of the house – cleaning, shopping and cooking. I'd done my best to be useful, sorting out all the technical stuff but, if I'd not been in such desperate straits, she'd hardly have bothered to employ any kind of assistant.

I'd given no thought as to what might happen when we got back. When it crossed my mind in my darker moments, I'd pushed the idea aside as I had no clue as to how I was going to solve it. Even if she kept me on for a few months longer, she was in no position to offer me a living wage. At the moment, I had free board and lodging, but the time was rapidly approaching when I was going to have to sort myself out once and for all.

The trouble was that jobs were scarce even for those offering only a minimum wage. I'd managed to get a couple of interviews, but I'd been told I was overqualified. Without a reference from the bank, there was no chance of another post in banking. Not that I wanted one. I'd had more than enough of a job I'd never wanted and had always found boring and unfulfilling. If it had been up to me, I'd have done a degree in graphic and media design, but mainly thanks to my own failure to stand up to Aunt Maud, I'd ended up doing accountancy.

A thin drizzle began to fall. The future did not look promising.

Time to make tracks. I picked up my bag and went in search of my mother to say goodbye.

It wasn't the best of journeys back to Aunt Jessica's. It was rush hour by the time the coach hit London and the underground was crowded.

'Hiya,' I called out as I pushed open the front door to Aunt Jessica's house.

'That you, Harry?' came a muffled voice from the kitchen.

'No. It's a burglar.'

I dropped my bag, hung up my coat and went to join her.

She was stirring a saucepan.

'I'll warm this up and then we can eat. I was expecting you back ages ago, sweetie.'

'The coach was late leaving Norwich and the traffic was horrendous.'

'You should have caught the train.'

I would have done if I'd had the money. Never had I missed my old car so much. I'd made the excuse that I wouldn't need it once I'd moved to London, but the real reason was I just couldn't afford to run it anymore. Road tax and the insurance would have been due next month, and the tyres looked as though at least two of them would fail the MOT next time around. Added to that, the engine had started to make some strange clunking sounds which suggested some very expensive repairs might be needed in the near future.

'So how was your visit? All well in sleepy Norfolk?'

'They're all in fine fettle and send their love.'

She turned back from the stove and pulled a face. 'I bet they did.'

'They did,' I protested. 'Well Mum did anyway. Aunt Edwina sent her regards and Aunt Maud said something about you should go and see them all soon.' What she'd actually said was to tell Jessica it was time she bothered to take time out from all her gallivanting all over the world and visit her sisters as they weren't getting any younger.

'Oh, for goodness sake, I went up at Christmas.' She turned back to her cooking. 'Right, you'd better take your things up to your room and get back here pretty smartish because I'm about to serve up. This stew's been kept warm for so long, it's a miracle it hasn't boiled itself dry.'

We ate in the kitchen. Aunt Jessica was not the world's greatest cook as she would be the first to admit, but there was not a lot you could do wrong with a basic stew.

'I'm glad you're back, sweetie; I've been living on beans on toast for the last three days.' I'd taken over the kitchen since I'd moved in. Apart from giving her more time to concentrate on her work, it happens to be one of my few talents. Perhaps I should look for a job in the catering industry.

We ate more or less in companionable silence and it wasn't until I was wiping around my plate with the toe end of my half of the garlic baguette that I glanced up and saw the searching look on her face.

'Are you going to tell me what's wrong?' she asked.

'What do you mean?'

'Most of the time I have a job to get a word in edgeways, but something's obviously upset you. You've hardly said a word since you got back.'

'I'm tired, that's all. Travelling always takes it out of me.'

Her eyes widened and she gave a derisive snort. 'I presume Maud had a go at you again, but you should be used to that, so what are you worrying about? The prospect of this trip to Japan has made you come alive these past few weeks. You left this house four days ago as confident and happy as I've ever seen you, but now you're back to that dejected loner you were when I took you in just before Christmas. I hope you're not going to be like a wet weekend when we get to Japan?'

I'm not good at expressing my feelings. Aunt Jessica is one of the few people with whom I feel I can be my real self and don't have to weigh up every word or put on a persona. Strange really as she's not exactly what you'd call a people person. Or perhaps that is the explanation. We're both outsiders, but in her case, she couldn't give a damn about how others see her. For as long as I've known her, she's always done and said whatever she feels.

'Sorry,' I said quickly, forcing a smile. 'I am excited about Japan, you know I am.'

She pushed her plate away, put her elbows on the table and cupping her chin in her hands, gave me her full attention. 'Spill.'

I gave a long sigh. 'It's just that on the journey back home, I've been giving some thought to what I'm going to do when we get back from Japan. We've been flat out getting everything ready for Tuesday, I've kept pushing it to the back of my mind.'

'I see. And what have you come up with?'

I shook my head. 'That's the trouble. Not an awful lot. I may not have been technically sacked from the bank, but HR made it clear that unless I handed in my resignation effective immediately, they would go through official dismissal procedures. Without a decent reference, there's no chance of another post in the banking world and I can't see how I could use my degree for any other decent job because they'd still want references of some kind. Any reputable company would.'

'So, you're going to have to think outside the box?'

'What does that mean?'

'You need to list all the things you're good at.'

'Such as? Figures and accounts are the only thing I know.'

'You'll think of something,' she said, pushing back her chair. 'But right now, I suggest we wash up the supper things and then sit down and work out what we need to do tomorrow. We've only got a couple more days before we leave, and I need to check the final details with the travel company, there's the handouts to print off and you'll need to collect the travel money.'

'Will do.'

'And we'd better make a start on the packing to check the cases aren't overweight. There's a strict luggage limit with no allowance for all the extra stuff I'll need for my talks.'

I nodded, picked up the dirty plates and carried them over to the sink. 'Okeydokey. I'd like to do a final check on the presentations and make copies on a couple of memory sticks as backup before we go.'

Since Aunt Jessica had taken me under her wing, my life had some purpose again. For the first time in over a year, I'd dared to hope that things had turned a corner. I think even at that point, I'd hoped she might turn round and tell me not to worry about what the future might hold because I'd be working for her indefinitely. But her next assignment with the travel company was over six months away and she'd managed perfectly well for years without an assistant before she'd invited me to join her. However, in a couple of weeks it looked as if I'd be back at square one again – jobless, maybe even homeless.

CHAPTER 2

We stayed at the table in the café until the departure boards flashed up the 'go to gate' sign. There was still more than half an hour until the plane was due to start boarding but already there were only a few seats left in the departure area.

'Are you keeping this seat for anyone or is it free?' I asked a burly-looking back-packer who had his legs stretched out across the narrow gap between the rows of seats.

With bad grace, he removed his rucksack, inevitably larger than the permitted size for cabin luggage, and I sat down. Aunt Jessica, barely able to hide the grin that threatened to erupt, took the seat next to me.

I raised an eyebrow, but she shook her head and began fishing in her bag for her magazine. Whatever had amused her she wasn't going to share it with me.

I looked around to see if I could spot any other distinctive red luggage labels like ours. At the far end of the row opposite sat a middle-aged couple attempting to change into their compression travel socks. Not the easiest thing to do with any elegance especially when middle-age spread has taken its toll on the waistline.

'I think those two are in our group,' I said to Aunt Jessica. 'See their luggage labels?'

She looked up and peered in the direction I'd indicated with a nod of my head.

'Hmm. You're probably right.' She went straight back to the article she was reading in her archaeology magazine.

I continued to study the couple. He was very red in the face, but whether that was due to his struggles with the socks or was his natural colouring, it was hard to tell. By the time he'd finished, there was a visible sheen on the skin exposed by his receding hairline. His wife made some comment, to which, to judge from the look on her face, he returned a none too polite reply. Not a good omen, but best to reserve judgement until I got to know them a little better. Travelling rarely brings out the best in people.

After the business class and families with small children were boarded, our group was called. It seemed that almost all the passengers got to their feet and the queue stretched back beyond the next gate. Nothing seemed to move and a good five minutes later we were still in the same spot.

Our backpacker with his three-day old beard came sauntering towards us clearly intent on finding a place where he could push in. I'm not a tactile person, I like my personal space, so I'd left a small gap behind the couple in front of me. I could see our would-be intruder eyeing the space. It would have been too pointed to have taken a step forward, so he decided to take full advantage.

'Excuse me,' I said politely as he tried to elbow his way in. 'The end of the queue is back there.'

He turned glowering down at me. He was a good four inches taller, so I had to peer up at him. Even though he was twice my weight, I refused to look intimidated.

'There's no need to be passive aggressive, Nancy Boy,' he sneered.

That did it. It's true I find myself more attracted to members of my own sex, but I certainly don't flaunt it. The expression he'd used was as offensive to me as any racist slur.

'You're mistaken,' I said quietly. He visibly relaxed. 'There's absolutely nothing passive about my aggression. Get. To. The. Back. Of. The. Queue.'

He was so surprised that he slunk off without another word.

The couple in front turned and smiled at me. 'Well done, you.'

My aunt gave a low chuckle. 'You'd never have done that two months ago, sweetie,' she whispered as she slipped her arm through mine.

I patted her hand and grinned. I did feel proud of myself, though heaven knows what I'd have done if he'd turned nasty.

It was an overnight flight, but I can't sleep on planes – not that I've had that much experience of flying. I dozed off for an hour or so but spent most of the time watching films. After the stewardess had taken away the remnants of our evening meal, Aunt Jessica tipped back her seat, nestled her travel pillow against the narrow stretch of wall next to the window, put on the eyeshade and slept, or made a decent job of resting.

Across from my aisle seat was another couple with red travel tags on their luggage. She was reading through some of the itinerary papers like the ones the company had sent us, so they were definitely in our party. They both settled down to sleep after dinner so there was no chance of introducing myself and getting to know them. That didn't stop me surreptitiously scrutinising them. They were younger than the other couple, late forties perhaps? From the little I'd overheard between them when we'd first got on the plane, I reckoned they came from up north somewhere. Nothing as recognisable as Liverpool or Newcastle accents, and from the few words I had managed to catch, I couldn't even be sure from which side of the Pennines they hailed. They looked healthy outdoor types, both dressed in stout walking shoes and she wasn't wearing any make-up. I couldn't see him as the type to work in an office and I wondered if they were perhaps farmers.

I settled back and flicked through the new releases in the inflight magazine until I found a film I fancied. Whatever problems on the job front that I needed to face in the future,

I refused to let them spoil this holiday. I'd been looking forward to it for two whole months and in any case, practically speaking, there was nothing I could do about it for the next fifteen days.

We arrived in Osaka in the early morning and met up with the rest of the British contingent in our party – the two couples we'd already spotted, plus two sisters and an attractive-looking man in his mid-to-late thirties. We all introduced ourselves. The older couple were Curtis and Isabel, the hardy types were Vincent and Gail, the two sisters were Lucy and Joanna and the single man introduced himself as Josh. We were all gathered up by an efficient-looking Japanese woman who led us to a minibus which was to drive us to our hotel in Kyoto.

The suburbs of Osaka were crammed with blocks of grey high-rise apartments and offices separated by narrow streets. I was hoping to get a feel for the country on the journey, but as we travelled on the main roads, it was much like any other motorway with little to see but cuttings and the occasional characterless warehousing and office blocks as we passed through built-up areas. We could have been anywhere back home. They even drove on the left like in Britain.

Once we'd checked into the hotel, we went straight to our rooms. It might be mid-morning Japanese time, but we both needed some sleep. I carried my aunt's case to her room and left her to unpack.

There was a welcome pack on the dressing table in my room. I took a quick look to see what time we were expected to be anywhere and was pleased to see our get-together meeting wasn't until five. I put the do-not-disturb notice on the door outside, closed the blinds, shrugged out of my clothes, decided I was much too tired for a shower and crawled under the duvet.

I slept until three. I took my time sorting myself out. Our stay in Kyoto was for three nights, so I picked out the clothes and other essentials I'd need, leaving everything else in the grip.

Time to check on Aunt Jessica. She'd already removed the do-not-disturb sign, so I knocked tentatively on her door. She looked a lot more refreshed than I felt. It was hard to believe she was in her mid-seventies. Her energy and enthusiasm – her whole outlook on life – never ceased to surprise me.

'We won't be eating till eight. Fancy going out to find somewhere for a bite?' I asked.

'Lead the way, sweetie,' she said, picking up her bag.

Following the directions the hotel receptionist had given us, we found a small café a few streets away.

'Can't say I'm that hungry, but I'd love a cup of good old English breakfast tea.'

'You'll be lucky,' she laughed. 'You'll have to get used to green tea or stick to coffee.'

'I don't mind green tea.'

'Hmm.' She pulled a face. 'I wouldn't be too sure. The Japanese stuff is nothing like you're used to in Chinese restaurants.'

'Coffee it is then,' I said as I held open the door for her to go in.

At five o'clock we went down to meet our tour manager and be introduced to the rest of our fellow passengers.

A group of half a dozen people were already sitting in a corner and a woman looked up from her clipboard, got to her feet and held out a hand.

'Now you two must be Jessica and Harry?' she said with a distinct Australian accent.

'Spot on,' I said. 'And you I take it, are Geraldine.' It wasn't hard to work out. The welcome note in our arrival pack had been signed by a Geraldine Hardy, tour manager.

'Call me Gerri.' Her shoulder length dark-brown hair was pulled back in a ponytail. 'We're going to leave the introductions until we all get here. No point in going through the process over and over. I'm just checking everyone has arrived.'

Apart from the other Brits we'd met in the airport, there was a couple from New Zealand and three more Australians – a married couple plus his brother.

They all seemed pleasant enough. There was quite an age range. The youngest, Lucy, one of the British sisters, was in her late twenties, and Aunt Jessica much the oldest.

Gerri gave us a rundown on the general programme and told us about the arrangements for that evening's meal.

'There's been a change of plan from what you have written in your itinerary notes. We were going for our Kaiseki meal in the Geisha district tomorrow, but there was a problem at the tea house, so we'll be going this evening. It promises to be a memorable experience.'

CHAPTER 3

'Have you ever had one of these Kaiseki meals before?' I asked my aunt as we made our way down in the lift. 'Sounds a bit airy-fairy to me. What did Gerri call it, a balance of taste, texture and appearance that blends into an art form? I hope there's not too much raw fish. I'm not at all sure about Japanese food.'

Aunt Jessica chuckled. 'I'm sure it will be fine. Where's your sense of adventure?'

I pulled a face. 'I'm a meat and two veg man at heart.'

'I don't know,' she gave a mock sigh. 'You can take the boy out of Norfolk, but you can't take Norfolk out of the boy. Just because my sisters still live in the nineteen sixties and have probably never even tasted a curry, there's no call for you not to widen your horizons.'

Though I had been brought up on traditional English fare when even pasta was regarded with suspicion, like every other student I'd lived on takeaway pizzas and curries. Before I could think of a clever retort, the lift doors opened at the second floor and several people, including the two sisters we'd met at the airport, squeezed in.

'You two look very pretty,' I said gallantly.

Lucy giggled looking a little self-conscious. She was dressed to the nines in a figure-hugging dress revealing a considerable amount of cleavage which I tried very hard not to stare at as she was pressed close to me in the crowded space.

'Thanks,' she said breathlessly. 'It's not too much is it?'

'Not at all. Perfect for the occasion,' I replied. Perhaps I should have found something smarter that my casual denim shirt and chinos.

As soon as the doors opened, the others all spilled out. I glanced at Aunt Jessica who was staring at me.

'What?'

She chuckled. 'Your face, sweetie. You looked like the proverbial rabbit caught in the headlights.'

For a moment I considered pretending I didn't know what she was talking about, but I knew my aunt only too well. 'That girl was trying to flirt with me!'

'I think she probably realises that you swing the other way, sweetie. A woman can sense these things.'

My cheeks were still burning as we made our way over to those in our party who were already waiting in one of the more secluded areas of the lobby. Aunt Jessica was immediately buttonholed by Curtis Benson, the guy we'd first seen at Heathrow airport putting on his travel socks. He'd been reading up about Samurai warriors on the plane coming over and he had some query he thought she might be able to help him with.

I wasn't comfortable being left in the company of the two girls. I looked around for Gerri, but she was busy talking with a Japanese girl.

'Do you think that's our local guide?' I said somewhat lamely as the two girls looked at me expectantly.

'Probably,' replied Lucy in a bored voice as she glanced round for someone else to talk to.

Josh the single chap from Britain arrived. He had what's frequently called rugged good looks – a square chin, well-shaped mouth and nose plus long eyelashes that any woman would be proud of. He smiled at us and the girls hurried over to speak to him.

He caught my eye as I stared at him and gave me a nod, as if to say I stood no chance with the girls when he was around.

Luckily, we didn't have to wait much longer as a minute or so later, the last of the party emerged from the lift.

'Right everyone,' Gerri called for attention. 'Now we're all here, let me introduce you to Aiko who'll be our local guide for the next three days while we're in Kyoto. As I said this afternoon, we'll take the minibus to the Geisha district, then walk to the tea house where we are going to eat and be entertained by a geisha.'

'Some people in the West have the mistaken idea that geisha are prostitutes which is not correct. The word geisha literally translates as performing artist. They are known for performing the ancient Japanese traditions of art, elegant and graceful dance, singing and demure conversation. The great attraction of the geisha world is its absolute discretion. All conversations that take place at the meetings are confidential. The relationship between geisha and client is strong and highly prized,' Aiko explained. 'The Japanese word ochaya translates as tea house, but it is not a place where they prepare and serve tea. It is the place where geisha entertain their clients. They are very exclusive establishments. Usually, one may enter only if one is already an established patron and only then with a reservation. Very few foreigners ever venture into a tea house and we are privileged that your company was able to arrange a visit. It only happens for a brief period for a few nights each year and then only for a small group of tourists.'

Our party were shown into a small traditional room with sliding paper panelled walls. Much to my relief, Aunt Jessica and I did not have to share a table with the two sisters. We sat with the two New Zealanders, Bruce and Molly Cowell.

All the food was already laid out on a tray at each place setting. Aiko came round to each table to explain what we had in front of us and the order in which it should be eaten.

'The raw fish you dip in the boiling water to cook before you eat it.'

'That's a relief,' I muttered.

As we were eating, we had a chance to get to know Bruce and Molly a little better. It turned out that they owned a dairy farm on South Island.

'What's happening to all your cows while you're away?' asked Aunt Jessica.

'We have an excellent foreman.'

I didn't pay much attention as Bruce and Aunt Jessica chatted away about changing farming patterns. Not because I wasn't interested, they were a pleasant friendly pair and we got on well, but because I was too busy trying to think what to say when the inevitable question came. One of them would be bound to ask what line of work I was in.

I was spared the problem because the door slid open and a tiny white-faced figure glided into the room followed by a somewhat grizzled elderly man. He was holding a stringed instrument resembling a lute with a small square box and a long thin neck.

After we'd all shuffled our chairs to get a good view of the girl, she gave us a deep bow.

'This is Excellent Jewel,' said Aiko. 'She is a maiko or trainee geisha. She is going to dance for us and then she will tell us a little about her life and her daily routine. After that, you will all have a chance to ask her any questions you may have.'

Her dancing was very slow and controlled. How she managed to twist and turn at all in the heavy silk embroidered kimono without getting her high platform sandals caught up in deep folds of material that lay all around her feet, I'll never know.

When she'd finished, she sank gracefully to the floor, sat back on her heels and arranged her skirts around herself. In a high singsong voice, she spoke for five minutes or so in Japanese stopping every few sentences for Aiko to translate for us.

Then the questions began in earnest.

'Did you always want to be a geisha?'

'Oh yes. For as long as I can remember. My parents

brought me to Kyoto as a small child and I saw the beautiful costumes and decided that is what I wanted to be.'

'What did your parents think about that? Did they try to dissuade you?'

She gave a charming little giggle which she hid behind her hand in a coy gesture.

'I bet that's part of her training,' I whispered in Aunt Jessica's ear.

'Why should they? It is a great honour to be chosen. When I auditioned to enter the okiya, my parents had to come with me and agree that they were happy for me to enter the geisha house.'

'Do you see them often?'

'Only twice a year.'

'Presumably, Excellent Jewel isn't your real name?' someone asked.

'We are all given a new name when we enter the geisha house.'

'Do you choose it?'

The young girl shook her head even before our guide translated the question. 'No. A maiko's name traditionally takes part of the name of her older geisha sister who looks after her.'

The women in her audience were interested in her kimono.

'There are different kimonos for each season. Each one can take two or three years to complete because of the painting and the embroidery. They are very expensive and are the property of the okiya.'

The questions kept coming and after fifteen minutes or so, Aiko told us there was time for one last question.

'How do you see your future? Would you like to establish your own geisha house?'

Again, Excellent Jewel gave a shy smile and dipped her head looking up from beneath her lashes. 'I would like to get married.'

Once she'd left, we rearranged our chairs and sat back at

our tables.

'I suppose becoming a geisha is one way to snag yourself a rich husband.'

'Bruce, you are such a cynic,' protested Molly.

'It stands to reason,' he protested. 'The only people she is ever going to meet from the outside world are her clients who are all very rich men.'

'He does have a point,' I laughed.

It would soon be time for us all to return to the hotel and people began to drift out to the washrooms. I decided to do the same.

The maze of dark, narrow passageways from the toilets back to our private room were lined with sliding paper doors. It all looked the same and had me totally confused. It didn't help that there was no one around to ask. It suddenly struck me, ever since our arrival, apart from Excellent Jewel and her accompanist, we had not seen any of the staff. I must have retraced my steps at least three times until I heard low voices off to one side at what I assumed must be the back of the building.

As I made my way towards the speakers to ask for directions, I heard a scuffle followed by a muffled cry. I hurried to the open doorway at the end of the corridor. In the dim light, I could just make out a black-clad figure with one forearm across a woman's shoulders forcing her against the wall. In his other hand he had a knife held at her throat.

'Hey,' I called out and rushed towards them.

I stopped short as he glanced at me over his shoulder. Before I could react, he turned back to the geisha, snarled something at her in Japanese then plunged the knife into her chest before running off in the other direction.

Her legs crumpled beneath her and her body slid slowly down the wall.

I tried to staunch the bleeding with my hands as best I could, but I'd seen enough drama on television to know that the worst thing I could do was to pull the knife out.

'Help, someone. We need help here,' I screamed at the top of my voice.

'Fox...you are here... key...important information...need to take it...tell no one.'

'Shush! Don't try to speak. Save your strength. Help will be here soon.'

Her eyelids drooped, and I started shouting again. I kept shouting until I heard footsteps running towards us.

'Harry, what on earth's the...' Aunt Jessica stood in the doorway.

'Get an ambulance, quick. She's been stabbed.'

It seemed ages before anyone else came.

Despite my best efforts, blood was still oozing through my fingers. I grabbed the end of her obi with one hand and tried to wrap the material around the blade, but the thick richly embroidered silk was too stiff to yield easily.

She was muttering something, but I was too busy trying to stem the bleeding, to work out what she was trying to say. One of her hands slipped out from under mine and she fumbled beneath the folds of the obi at her waist.

'Lie still now. Help will be here soon.'

'Take it...' She put her hand on my chest. 'Tell no one...give only to White Tiger...must take care...Water Dragon dangerous.'

Suddenly, Aunt Jessica was back accompanied by two of the staff. They all rushed over, but it was too late. The glint in her eyes faded and the red-painted lids drooped. I felt the tiny hand beneath my own go limp.

I'm not sure how long I remained with my hands still pressed to her chest. Not until a firm hand rested on my shoulder and my aunt's voice said softly, 'She's gone, Harry. You can let her go. There's nothing more you can do.'

I let my hands fall and sat back on my heels. Tears pricked at the back of my eyes. She was such a tiny figure. Whatever had she done to deserve such a fate?

There was more commotion as I got to my feet. Other people began to arrive. Excellent Jewel appeared in the doorway.

'Tamaryô!' Shouting at the top of her voice, she pushed her way but before she could fling herself on the recumbent figure, Aunt Jessica tried to catch hold of her. Excellent Jewel pulled away and swung round to me. She rushed at me screaming in Japanese and pounded her fists on my chest.

I was taken by surprise. My hands were covered in blood and I could do nothing to hold her off. She continued to force me back until we both began to fall. Aunt Jessica pulled her off me and one of the staff helped me to my feet.

'Shush, now. Shush.' My aunt enveloped the young maiko in her arms until the hysterical sobbing quietened down.

'She was my one-san, my older sister.' Her eyes blazing, she turned and pointed to me. 'Him! He stab her. He kill Jewel of Happiness!'

'No,' said Aunt Jessica calmly. 'He tried to save her.'

'Look,' she wailed. 'Blood on hands.'

'Because he tried to stop the bleeding. He had no reason to kill her.'

Excellent Jewel put her hands to her face and began crying again softly.

Suddenly she looked up. 'But why she here? Jewel of Happiness have no client this night. Not till Friday.'

It was not a question anyone could answer.

CHAPTER 4

Inspector Hamamoto was as inscrutable as the Japanese always appear to be. He was meticulously polite, but I couldn't help feeling that I was his number one suspect. Though what possible motive he thought I could have for murdering a woman I'd never met before was beyond me.

I was made to go over what I had seen several times. As the only description I could give of Jewel of Happiness's killer was that he was Japanese and dressed in black clothes with a scarf knotted at the back of his head, I couldn't give him much to go on.

'How tall was he?'

'Hmm. I'm not sure. Medium height. A little shorter than me.'

The sergeant, standing silently by the wall took notes.

'Age?'

'I only caught a fleeting glimpse of his face as he looked at me over his shoulder. He disappeared as soon as I got there. From the speed he ran away, I doubt he was an old man.'

'Could you identify him if we showed you some photographs?'

I shook my head. 'He was gone in seconds. She was still alive, so all my attention was trying to help her rather than on him.'

'No one else saw this man.' I wasn't sure if this was a question or a statement.

'As I said, when I heard someone cry out, I ran to see what was happening. There was no one else around.'

'Did she say anything?'

'I think she was trying to tell me something, but the words didn't make much sense. I think the loss of blood had made her light-headed. In any case, I was concentrating on trying to stop the bleeding rather than listening.'

'Could she have been trying to give you the name of her attacker?'

I shook my head. 'I don't think so. It was difficult to make out anything she was saying, something about information and a tiger, but I definitely didn't hear anything that sounded like a name.'

He didn't look convinced.

'I think that's enough questions for now, Inspector. The poor boy is absolutely exhausted, and he's been through a traumatic experience.'

Aunt Jessica had insisted on staying with me. It was only an informal questioning in a quiet room in the tea house rather than a proper interview at the police station, so he had no grounds for refusing her.

Inspector Hamamoto studied my aunt for a good thirty seconds as she stared him down before wisely deciding he had met his match. Short of dragging me off to the station, there was little more that he could do.

'That will be all for now, Mr Hamilton-James. However, we may need to speak to you again. If you do recall anything that may help in our enquiries, please do not hesitate to get in touch.'

'I will, Inspector.'

'And you have nothing more to add to your statement Miss Hamilton?'

'No. I came running when I heard Harry shouting for help. I saw him on the ground trying to staunch the blood. He told me to fetch an ambulance. Which I did. By the time I returned, the poor girl was dead.'

'Can you explain why you heard your nephew calling for

help when no one else did? What were you doing at the back of the building?'

'Harry and I left our dining room at the same time to visit the washrooms before our return journey. He still wasn't back five minutes after I'd returned so I went to find him. You can check with the others. I asked if any of the men in our group had seen him and Martin said Harry was just leaving as he went in. He was surprised he wasn't back.'

I could see the Inspector's brain ticking over. I obviously had more than enough time to find Jewel of Happiness, talk with her before finally stabbing her.

Aunt Jessica got to her feet.

'If that is all, Inspector. It's time for us to get back to our hotel.'

'I will arrange some transport for you both.'

'Thank you, Inspector. That will be much appreciated.'

We said very little in the car on the way back. Thankfully, it was unmarked. I did not fancy having to explain why we were returning to the hotel in a police car. I'd cleaned myself up in the washroom before my interview with the inspector, but the cuffs of my shirt were soaked in blood and the sleeves and shirtfront were covered in splatter. Luckily, I'd left my jacket on the back of the chair in the dining room and was able to cover up the worst of the damage, but the knees of my trousers were stained a dark brick red. Getting from the door to my room without causing comment was going to be a difficult task.

'I hope there's no one about. I don't fancy having to explain how I got in this state,' I muttered as the car pulled up outside the hotel.

'I doubt there'll be many people still up at this hour.'

Our driver was out of the car and holding the door open for me the moment we stopped. He gave a deep bow and had sped off before we'd barely had time to thank him.

Whether it was delayed shock or just sheer exhaustion, my limbs suddenly felt stiff and heavy and Aunt Jessica took me by the arm to steady me as we mounted the low half dozen steps to the glass entrance doors.

The large foyer was empty of guests and, with my aunt on my right shielding me from the view of the receptionist at the desk beyond the flight of open-plan stairs, we covered what seemed an interminable distance to the lift at the fastest pace I could muster. We made my room without incident and I sank down on the edge of the bed.

'You look done in.' She bent down to take off my shoes for me.

'You'd better give me that shirt. I'll put it in some cold water before it gets stained for good.'

She helped me off with it then frowned. 'Those trousers are covered in blood so off with them as well.'

'What now?'

'Don't be such a prude. Unless you're not wearing underpants, of course.'

She took my clothes and disappeared into the bathroom. I grabbed a pair of jeans from the wardrobe and pulled on yesterday's shirt then lay back and closed my eyes, but my mind was racing. I kept going over all that had happened.

'I've rinsed the worst of it off and left your things soaking in the sink. Once you've had your shower, you can hang them up in there overnight.'

'Will do,' I said as I struggled back up to a sitting position.

'You left this in the breast pocket of your shirt. Silly place to put your luggage key.'

I stared at it. 'But it's not mine.'

'Are you sure? It looked like the one for the little padlock you've got on your grip.'

'It does. But mine's on my keyring.' I pointed to the pile of things she'd emptied from my trouser pockets and dropped on the bedside table.

'Then how did it get there?'

'Heaven knows. It was a brand-new shirt. Tonight was the first time I'd worn it and it definitely wasn't there when I

31

put it on.'

'How could someone put it there without you realising?'

'I really don't know.'

Aunt Jessica sat down on the bed next to me. After a moment or two of silence, she said. 'There were blood marks all down the front of your shirt. Could the geisha have put it there?'

'She was the only one close enough I suppose, but...' I shook my head. 'I really don't know. She said something... I might have heard the word key. I'm not sure... I can't think. I wasn't really listening. She was saying all sorts of things but none of it made much sense. I thought she was just rambling.'

'In English or Japanese?'

I looked at her. 'I don't understand.'

'If she was rambling, she'd have been talking in her own language. If it was in English, she was trying to tell you something. Something important. She must have realised she was dying so you need to try and remember what she said.'

What my aunt said made sense, but my mind was a blank.

'Close your eyes. Think back to when you first saw her.'

'She said something like, "Fox, you've come," and she seemed relieved I was there.'

'Fox?'

'She said it several times. I think that was her name for me. Just before she died, she said, "Listen, Fox." At least, I think that's what she was trying to say.'

'Listen to what?'

'By then her voice was very weak. I only caught the odd word. Something about find a White Tiger at some shrine.'

'Which shrine?'

'As I keep saying, I wasn't really paying much attention. It might have been Itsu something.' I screwed my eyes closed again trying to recall her voice. 'I do remember her saying, "Beware of the Water Dragon". But none of that makes sense. It was just her dying rambles.'

Aunt Jessica didn't look so convinced. After a moment or

two, she asked, 'Is that it?'

I nodded and I let out a long sigh.

Aunt Jessica patted me on the shoulder and stood up. 'It's very late. Take a shower and get to bed or you'll never be ready for the morning. I've no idea what time we're meeting, but we can find out at breakfast.'

In a rare gesture of affection, she bent down and kissed the top of my head.

'Night-night. Sweet dreams.'

CHAPTER 5

Despite my earlier exhaustion, it was some time before I could get to sleep. The picture of the dying woman's face kept coming back – the pleading look in those dark eyes. I could hear the urgency in her voice even though, try as I might, I could remember little of what she had said. Even the few words I did recall didn't make any sense.

I must have dropped off eventually because the alarm on my phone woke me at 7.15. After a long hot shower and despite having had no more than five hours sleep, I felt surprisingly refreshed. We returned to the hotel well after midnight and my aunt and I had talked for over an hour.

Aunt Jessica knocked on my door just before eight o'clock.

'You ready for some breakfast, sweetie?'

'Uh-huh. Though whether I'm ready to face everyone else's questions, is another matter.'

She laughed. 'You'll cope. You have to face them all sometime.'

They were nearly all there. Even those who'd already eaten were standing around the tables still talking.

'What happened to you two?' demanded Bruce. 'We were all worried about the pair of you. The police said there'd been an incident and we had to stay where we were for the

34

time being.'

'We knew something serious had happened,' added Molly, his wife. 'They wanted to know where we all were throughout the evening, but they wouldn't answer any of our questions.'

'Eventually they came back and said we could go,' Gerri said. 'I explained we couldn't leave without you two because you'd have no way to get back to the hotel. The policeman said, not to worry, they would arrange transport for you both.'

'We assumed that meant you must be alright, but why on earth wouldn't they let you join us?'

'We wondered what you'd done to get on the wrong side of the law. Why else would they question you for so long?' said Vincent with a laugh. 'So why did they keep you?'

'This morning, we heard that someone had been attacked. One of the other hotel guests said someone had been stabbed in the Geisha District and asked if we knew anything about it.'

'For goodness sake,' interrupted Isabel Benson, the motherly woman we'd first spotted at Heathrow airport. 'Let them both get themselves some breakfast before you start bombarding them with questions.'

'Good idea,' said Aunt Jessica. 'I'm starving.'

As we helped ourselves at the buffet, Isabel and Gail, the other English woman brought cups of coffee for us to our table. I'd like to say they were just being helpful, but I had a sneaking suspicion that it was only to speed up the process before they all began pumping us for more information about what had happened at the tea house.

Aunt Jessica and I had agreed in the lift coming down that we would make as light of the whole affair as possible. Without actually telling an outright lie, I explained I'd heard a scream and went to see what was happening and I found a woman who'd been stabbed. I called for help and Aunt Jessica had gone to ring for an ambulance.

'So, who was it?'

'She was dressed like a geisha.'

'Not our girl, was it?'

'No,' I reassured Isabel. 'It definitely wasn't Excellent Jewel. We hadn't seen the poor woman before.'

'Did they take her to hospital?'

'The police arrived almost as soon as the paramedics got there,' my aunt said firmly. 'Obviously they wanted to talk to us about what we'd seen so they took us to another room.'

The questions went on for some time. My coffee was stone cold by the time I had a chance to drink it, so I went for another cup. By the time I got back, the group had been joined by a very animated Heather and Martin Stratford, the Australian couple.

'We've just been talking to the girls who clean our rooms. There were three of the them in a cluster blocking the end of the corridor.'

'They were so busy nattering, they didn't notice us at first and Martin had to ask them to let us through.'

'Anyway,' Martin frowned at his wife's interruption. 'One of them asked if we were in the group who were at the tea house where a geisha was murdered. They told us it was the second murder in the city this month.'

'Was that another geisha?' asked Gail. 'You hear about these maniacs who think they've been given a mission to rid the town of prostitutes.'

'No nothing like that. This was some businessman.'

'I thought Japan was supposed to be a safe country,' Isabel said with a worried frown.

Gerri put an arm around her shoulder. 'It is. It has one of the lowest crime rates in the world. Kyoto especially. There is nothing for you to worry about. I've been living here for seven years now and this is the first time I've heard of anything like this.'

As Gerri led her away, the others dispersed either to get more food from the buffet table or return to their rooms.

At least it took the pressure off me.

There wasn't much time to get ready by the time we got back to our rooms. I cleaned my teeth, collected what I'd need for the day's outing and went next door to Aunt Jessica's.

'I think that's everything.' She stuffed a plastic mac into her bag and hoisted the strap onto her shoulder.

'Camera.' I pointed to the camera bag on the bed.

'Ah. Not sure I want to be bothered with it today. I've no plans to do any research on this trip so I don't really need it. Here, you take it. You'll get much better results than trying to take snaps on your phone.'

She thrust it into my hands and made for the door before I had a chance to reply. 'Come on now or we'll be late. Mustn't keep everyone waiting.'

I had a shrewd suspicion that she was just trying to take my mind off last night's events. There was a time when I was really interested in photography, but I'd had to sell all my equipment some time back when money became tight. She knew how much I coveted her top-of-the-range equipment. Aunt Jessica was something of an expert. She needed to be for her work, first as an archaeologist and more recently writing her travel articles for some of the upmarket travel magazines.

'Kyoto is the spiritual capital of Japan. We have more than 1,000 temples and shrines…'

I did my best to concentrate on Aiko's spiel as our minibus drove us to the north of the city to visit the famous Golden Temple which Aiko assured us was one of Japan's most treasured sites, but it wasn't easy.

The temple was set on a wooded hill. The grounds were extensive, and it was a long walk to get to a spot around the lake from where we could take the best photos. According to Aiko, it was built in 1397 as a retirement villa for a powerful shogun but after his death, it was converted into a zen temple as he had commanded in his will. It burnt down several times in its history, most recently in 1950 when it was set on fire by a mad novice monk.

'Makes a good picture, with the sun sparkling on the roof like that, you have to admit,' said Chandler Stratford in his slow Aussie drawl. It was impressive. Its top two floors were covered in gold leaf.

We were standing elbow to elbow at the railing, cameras raised.

'I'm trying to get the reflection in the water without that bit of scaffolding showing.'

We talked cameras for a while, but I guessed the real reason for him striking up a conversation with me was to ask about last night.

The rest of the group began to follow the guide leading the way to the gardens behind the temple. Chandler seemed in no hurry to join his brother and sister-in-law and hung back so that our conversation could not be overheard.

'Pretty heroic stepping in last night to try and stop that poor woman being attacked. You were lucky he didn't turn the knife on you.'

'Not really. He ran away as soon as I turned the corner.'

'You weren't to know that's what he'd do.'

'All I did was to shout at him. It's what anyone would have done.'

'Did the police catch him, do you know?'

'They didn't take me into their confidence,' I said dismissively, trying to quicken my pace to catch up with the others.

Either he failed to take the hint or chose to ignore it because he went on, 'I wonder why he did it. It could have been personal. Some grievance or other. You can't just waltz into those places. The security is pretty tight because of all their high-profile clients, so it stands to reason he probably worked there. Or she may have spotted him doing something he shouldn't and had to be silenced.'

The same ideas had been going round in my head in the small hours.

'You may well be right. I don't suppose we'll ever know. Shall we catch up with the others?'

CHAPTER 6

For the rest of the visit, I stayed close to Aunt Jessica. I had no intention of getting button-holed by Chandler again or anyone else for that matter. The least said about last night the better as far as I was concerned.

We were taken to see the oldest bonsai tree in Kyoto. It was outside what our guide called the tea house.

'I thought bonsai trees were supposed to be miniature. That's as tall as the building,' I whispered to my aunt as we all gathered round listening to Aiko's patter. 'And it's an odd sort of shape.'

Aunt Jessica wrinkled her nose and gave me a mock glower. 'Okay, Mr Grumpy; who's been rattling your cage?'

'Well, if you must know...' I told her about Chandler pumping me about last night's events.

She looked thoughtful. 'I can appreciate you didn't want to talk to him about what happened, but, by the sound of it, he did raise some very interesting questions. Why would anyone want to kill Jewel of Happiness, and how did our assassin get into the tea house? I presume the police will have interviewed all the staff.'

For the next half hour, we were free to wander and explore the gardens and the mirror pond on our own, so we were able to continue our discussion without fear of being overheard.

'And I've got another question. When Chandler was pumping me earlier, another thought struck me. You know I told you that Jewel of Happiness kept talking about a fox?'

'You decided that was her name for you.'

'Exactly. It was as though she knew I was coming. She assumed I knew all about the key. Why else would she give it to me? She must have thought I knew exactly what to do with it otherwise she'd have told me what it was for. So, my question is, who is the real Fox?'

'Hmm. Good question.' Aunt Jessica stopped walking and stood with her head on one side, a slight frown of concentration on her forehead. 'Presumably, this Fox character must be English-speaking.'

'Even I had worked that out.' I'd been hoping she'd come up with something a little more enlightening.

We carried on walking and after a few moments, she said, 'Excellent Jewel was surprised to see the geisha there at all. According to our young maiko, Jewel of Happiness had no customers at the tea house for the next couple of evenings.'

'So?'

'Our visit to the tea house was brought forward at the last minute. According to the original itinerary, it should have been Friday on our last evening in Kyoto.'

'I still don't see the connection.'

'What if the original plan was for Jewel of Happiness to meet up with Fox on the Friday, but the sudden change of plan meant she had to come in last evening instead?'

'You think Fox must be one of our group?'

'Let's just say, the little evidence we have rather suggests it. Fox couldn't have been one of her regular clients otherwise she would have recognised him. She spoke to you in English and there were no other English-speaking people in the establishment. We were the only party there.'

'So, when I appeared, she assumed I'd come to look for her?'

'Can you think of any other explanation?'

'But who in our group could it have been? Is that why Chandler was trying to wheedle information out of me? Could he be the real Fox?'

'It could just as easily have been one of the others. It would help if we knew exactly what that key is supposed to open. We have no idea what all this is about and exactly what role Fox is supposed to play in it.'

In the afternoon we were taken to Nijo castle, built in 1603 as the residence of Tokugawa Ieyasu, the first in a whole line of shoguns who were to rule Japan for the next two and half centuries. I knew quite a bit about this legendary character from the PowerPoint presentation I'd put together from Aunt Jessica's notes. He had become one of my favourite historical figures. Back in the late sixteenth century, the country had an ineffective emperor who was more interested in pursuing his own pleasures in his luxury palace in the company of his favourites and hangers-on, than in running a country. Tokugawa took control and turned what had been a collection of feudal warring samurai fiefdoms into a united, forward-looking nation.

Visiting his castle and walking on its nightingale floors was high on my bucket list. I was fascinated by the idea that in order to prevent an unknown assassin from sneaking up on him unawares, Ieyasu had the floors specially designed so that the boards would creak sounding like birds singing whenever anyone stepped on them.

The moment we passed under the spectacular towering wooden entrance gate with its intricately patterned tiered roof picked out in gold leaf, I was entranced. So much so, all the tension of the previous night disappeared as I wandered down the corridors admiring the painted screens and imagining the splendour of the audiences in the large hall where the samurai lords were summoned to pay homage. Here, even the emperor sat on a lower dais than the shogun himself.

Once we left the building, we were free to explore the castle grounds by ourselves. Aunt Jessica tucked her arm in mine, and we made for the small artificial lake. Filled with rocky outcrops, it was a picturesque site. I must have taken thirty photos before my aunt had had enough.

'If we stay here much longer, there won't be time to see the cherry groves.'

I fell into step and we wandered on.

Every shade of pink blossom cascaded like curtains from the trees. A photographer's paradise. To complete the picture, scores of beautiful young women clad in richly embroidered kimonos tottered past us on their traditional ridiculously high platform sandals. The town was full of shops which hired out costumes by the day.

Aunt Jessica gave a low chuckle. 'Now that epitomises Japan. A perfect blend of traditional and ultra-modern.'

I turned to see what she was looking at. A girl in a white flowered kimono, her long black hair swept on top of her head and held in place with flowers, was standing in the trees framed by a drooping branch heavy with blossom, taking her own photo with a long selfie stick.

It was as we were walking back to the meeting point that Aunt Jessica said, 'Don't look round, but we are being followed. I said don't look.' Her grip tightened painfully on my arm as I started to turn my head.

'What does he look like?'

'There're are two of them. Not together. They take it in turns to hang back. I presume that's to make it less obvious though it actually has the opposite effect. One's youngish, wearing jeans and a grey zip-up jacket and there's an older man in dark clothes and wearing glasses.'

'Are you sure they're interested in us?'

'They were following the group this morning at the Golden Temple.'

'I didn't notice anyone.'

'You've been too busy taking pictures. I presume that's what they were banking on.'

I stopped at one of the drink machines and took my time selecting a can and drinking its contents. It gave me an excellent opportunity not only to turn and look behind me, but to see if the men continued to walk on whilst I stood there drinking my lemonade.

I took a good look at the younger man as he strolled past. 'Where is the other one?'

'Stopped back there. Taking photos.'

'Are you sure? Why would anyone want to follow us?'

'The only thing I can think of is that it has something to do with what happened at the tea house last night.'

'What should we do, do you think?'

'Short of tackling him, there's not much you can do.'

'He'd just deny it if I did. Even if he admitted being at the Golden Temple, there must be dozens of tourists here now who were there this morning. They are two of the most popular sites in Kyoto.'

'Exactly. Let's just see if they're at our next stop.'

CHAPTER 7

The minibus was not the place to air private matters and there was no time to discuss our two mystery followers when we first got back to the hotel. Aunt Jessica had to get ready for her first talk on the history of Kyoto and its role as Japan's cultural capital. The presentation went well and there were several questions at the end. As yet more hands shot up, Aunt Jessica said, 'I think we'd better call a halt there. Gerri will be expecting us in the lobby in fifteen minutes, but I'm happy to answer any more questions later. It's not as though I'm rushing off anywhere. We have the rest of the holiday together.'

As everyone drifted away and Aunt Jessica and I started packing away the laptop and cables, Curtis, the older British guy, came up. 'Can I just say how much I enjoyed your talk, Jessica.'

'Thank you for saying so.'

'I was fascinated by your slides and how you incorporated that little bit of video into the presentation. Very impressive.'

Aunt Jessica gave him a beaming smile. 'I can't take any credit for that I'm afraid. It's Harry here who's the technical whizz. He put it all together for me and he's in the process of building me a new website.'

'Really?' He turned to me. 'Is that your line of work?'

'Not really. It's actually not that difficult to do,' I said and turned back to the projector unplugging its leads.

'Then you must give me a few tips some time.'

'I'd be happy to.'

'But not now, Curtis,' said his wife firmly from the doorway where she was hovering. 'We need to go and get ready.'

'Yes of course, dear. And I mustn't hold up you two good people. Thank you again. I'm really looking forward to your next talk.'

With that he scuttled after his wife and I collected up the unused handouts left on the tables.

'I think you can put that down as a success.'

'Yes. I have to admit, Harry, I'm glad I let you persuade me to put everything up on PowerPoint. The pictures and the maps made it much easier to get things across.'

I tidied away the last of the extension leads, picked up the computer bag and looked around. 'Is that everything? If this is all there is, shall I run them back to my room for now and you can go straight down to the lobby?'

'No. I'll come too, then I can put the laptop in my room safe straight away.'

In the event, we hadn't kept everyone waiting. We were not the last downstairs. It was another five minutes before Lucy and her sister Joanna arrived, both dressed more for a party than a casual meal in a local restaurant with their short skirts and low-cut tops and swathed in floaty wraps. Lucy's long fair hair was swept up and held by a sparkly butterfly clip. I hoped for their sakes, we weren't going to be walking too far given the height of the heels of their strappy sandals.

Gerri explained, 'Most Japanese restaurants don't really cater for large groups. I'm going to take you to where we'll find the most eating places. What I'd suggest is you can look in the window at what's on offer and you can pick what you fancy. All the dishes are shown plated up so when you go in, you can just point to want you want.'

Gerri led the way, Aunt Jessica and I tagged on to the end of the crocodile following in her wake. Before long, we fell into conversation with Vincent and Gail, the couple who'd been sitting across the aisle from me on the plane coming over.

'I thought in Japanese restaurants you all sat at long tables surrounding the chap doing the actual cooking in the middle,' said Gail.

'I think you'll find very few like the sushi and tempura restaurants you find back home,' said Aunt Jessica. 'Some do have narrow counters where you can perch on a high stool and watch the chefs, but most have tables like back home designed for tourists. Though some sections are up on platforms with low tables and the diners sit on cushions, so best avoided unless you're happy to sit crossed-legged for an hour or so.'

'You obviously know Japan well. Have you been here often?' Vincent asked her.

'Not at all,' my aunt replied with a soft laugh. 'I came a few times with Professor Peverell in the 1980s, mainly for conferences, when we were doing archaeological work in this part of the world. We combined it with a bit of a holiday which included Kyoto before coming back to Britain, but things have changed a great deal since then.'

'I see.'

As the three of them chatted away, my mind drifted back to the question of whether our geisha's mystery Fox could be one of our party? Chandler Stratford was not the only single guy on the trip. Josh Rutherford, the British guy who thought he was God's gift, had also come on his own. Almost as soon as we'd left the hotel, the two Parkes sisters had button-holed him, one on either side. I tried to remember if I'd seen them all at the same table at the tea house the previous evening, but I hadn't been paying that much attention.

We ended up in a kind of shopping mall with eight or nine different eateries all within a short distance of each other. As Gerri had promised, the windows had display shelves with all the meals laid out.

'I expected pictures of the meals, not plastic food all

plated up like that,' I said to Aunt Jessica.

'See anything you like?'

Like most of the others, we wandered from one restaurant window to the next inspecting the wares. It took some time.

'Surely you've seen something that takes your fancy?' Aunt Jessica was beginning to get impatient. 'It will be midnight before eat at this rate.'

'I like to know what I'm eating, and I can't recognise what's on any of these plates.'

'For goodness' sake, Harry.' She only called me by my name on those rare occasions when she was cross with me. 'You're in Japan. How can you appreciate the culture if you don't at least *try* some of the cuisine? Where's your sense of adventure?'

I made a quick choice.

Inside, the place was almost full, but Vincent and Gail were already sitting at a table and invited us to join them.

My early assessment that these two came from somewhere up north turned out to be correct, but they were not farmers, not even country folk. He was a history teacher in a community college in Wakefield and she was a ward sister in the town's hospital. However, I was right about them being outdoor types as we soon discovered, they belonged to a local fell walking group.

I probably wasn't exactly the life and soul of the party that evening. It wasn't only that my thoughts kept returning to the identity of Fox, but any talk of what people did for a living put me on the defensive. However I dressed it up, explaining why my ten-year career in the banking industry came to an abrupt and inglorious end was never easy. I could hardly explain I had been effectively sacked for sexual harassment. That was how the bosses liked to put it, but the truth of what happened was in fact very different. If it hadn't had been for a homophobic colleague, the whole affair would never have come to light.

'Harry?'

'Sorry?'

'Gail asked you if something was wrong with your meal,' said my aunt.

I stared down at my plate and realised I'd only eaten a few mouthfuls and everyone else had almost finished.

'No, it's fine. Very good, actually. My mind was on other things.'

'Evidently,' Aunt Jessica said with a disapproving glare. 'You totally ignored Gail.'

'I'm so sorry,' I said quickly.

'It's perfectly understandable. After that horrible experience at the tea house last night, you must be quite traumatised.'

'Exactly,' added Vincent. 'Was the poor woman able to tell the police who attacked her?'

I shook my head. 'Sadly no. She was dead by the time they arrived.'

'She wasn't able to tell you?' he persisted.

'I'm afraid she collapsed straight away.'

'At least you were able to give them a description of the culprit.'

'Not really. He disappeared the moment I reached the doorway to the room.'

Aunt Jessica came to my rescue. 'Shall we change the subject to something a little less gruesome?'

'Excellent idea,' Gail agreed. 'Did you get some good photos today, Harry? Every time I spotted you, you were busy with your camera.'

Most of the party were keen on having an early night and it wasn't late by the time we got back to the hotel. Despite the lack of sleep over the last forty-eight hours, I knew there was no point in my going to bed until I'd had a chance to talk over the things buzzing around my brain with Aunt Jessica.

'Vincent seemed keen on finding out if our geisha told me anything before she died, don't you think?'

Aunt Jessica gave me a knowing smile. 'I'm not sure you

should read anything into that. I think most of the group are dying to ask you for more details. Some are better at hiding their prurient curiosity than others. While you were busy taking photos just before lunch, Lucy and Joanna were trying to pump me. I don't suppose you noticed.'

'But if Jewel of Happiness mistook me for this Fox character, doesn't that mean it must be a man?'

'Not necessarily. She had obviously never met Fox previously and if all she had was a code name, it could have been anyone.'

'What I don't understand is, why doesn't Fox come and identify him or herself? If whoever it is thinks I may have the key, why not come and ask for it?'

'Exactly. I've been pondering that little conundrum all day. Until we know what this whole business is really about, it's difficult to work out. It's like having a few pieces of a jigsaw with no picture or edge bits to help start putting them together. We've made the assumption that Jewel of Happiness was one of the good guys and whoever killed her was one of the baddies, but is it all as simple as that? She obviously got hold of something highly sensitive that's locked away somewhere, but we have no idea what it is or where.'

'And her killer was attempting to take whatever it was. Or the key if he knew it was locked away,' I suggested.

'Was he trying to steal it or get it back?'

I shook my head. 'Heaven knows.'

'So, what do you want to do about it?'

'What do you mean?'

'Are you going to hand over the key to the police and leave it all to them, push the whole affair to the back of your mind and get on an enjoy the rest of the holiday or…?'

'Or what?'

'Exactly!'

It was some time before I answered. 'My instinct is not to tell the police, but I can't explain why. What do you think I should do?'

49

'It's your decision, sweetie. Jewel of Happiness gave the key to you which presumably means she didn't want it to fall into anyone else's hands. However, practically speaking, where do you go from here? All you have is a key, but no knowledge of what it opens, and a multitude of questions with no idea where to look for answers.'

'Put like that...' I gave a long sigh.

'It's getting late. I suggest you sleep on it. We have another busy day tomorrow.'

As I got to the door, another thought struck me. 'I forgot to ask, did you notice those two who you thought might be following us at Nijo Castle at the shrine afterwards?'

'Not those two, no.'

'What does that mean?'

'Either I was mistaken earlier, or their replacements may have been a little more adept at making sure they weren't spotted.'

'That doesn't exactly fill me with a great deal of confidence.'

'Never fear, sweetie. I've got your back covered. Let's see what tomorrow brings.'

I returned to my own room telling myself that, in the past on her archaeology digs, Aunt Jessica had learnt to handle herself in some pretty tight spots in some very dangerous parts of the world. If the rumours were true, she'd tangled with bigtime smuggling gangs on more than one occasion. Though on which side, I had no idea. I'd never had the courage to ask.

CHAPTER 8

After breakfast on Friday, we set out to Arishiyama, a wooded hilly area on the western outskirts of the city. Gerri led us down a steep path lined with soaring bamboo trees.

'This is all a bit spooky; don't you think?' Molly asked of no one in particular. She stopped and looked around, a deep frown creasing her forehead. 'I'm not sure I like the feeling of being hemmed in by all these giant stems. You can't see more than a few feet into the forest and when you look up, you can hardly see the sky.'

Bruce tucked his wife's arm through his with a chuckle. 'What's to be nervous about?'

'I'm used to open spaces …'

I hung back and let the couple catch up with the rest of the group. I looked behind me, but ours was the only group in sight. If our stalkers were around today, they'd be hard pushed to follow us here.

It was a different matter at our next stop at the Ginkakuji shrine where the paths surrounding the Silver Temple were crowded with people.

'Spotted anyone following?' I asked Aunt Jessica.

'Difficult to tell, but at least with all these people around there's no need to feel you are under any threat.'

'I don't,' I protested. 'I was just wondering why they're bothering to follow us at all?'

'I would think because of what happened at the tea

house, wouldn't you?'

'I realised that,' I said crossly. 'I meant why me?'

She shrugged. 'If they suspect you have the key, they may be trying to see if you slope off somewhere to use it, perhaps.'

'But how would they know she gave the key to me? I'm not Fox. Wouldn't they be following the real Fox?'

'They may assume that it must be you because you were the one who found her.'

'And how would they know that? I thought the geisha world was all about secrecy and discretion.' I gave the matter more thought. 'I suppose her killer saw me.'

'You're not letting your imagination run away with you, are you?' She tucked her arm in mine. 'If it's any consolation, if I thought you were in serious danger, I'd have you on the plane back to Heathrow before you had time to phone home.'

I patted her hand. 'I don't doubt it.'

It wasn't that I thought for one moment that she didn't have my best interests at heart. Feisty she may have been but, when it came down to it, what kind of protection could I expect from a seventy-three-year-old woman?

In the afternoon, we were taken to the Philosopher's Walk, a picturesque path lined with cherry trees that stretched alongside the canal. We were given a couple of hours to explore the area and the various shrines by ourselves. Aunt Jessica's suspicions about us being followed had made me jittery so we decided that I would stop and take my time shooting photos giving her the opportunity to casually look around as she stood about waiting for me.

Halfway along the route, we sat on a bench by one of the shrines. It provided not only a good viewing point but a chance to talk without fear of being overheard by anyone coming up behind without us realising it.

'Have you given any more thought to what you want to do?'

'Yes, quite a bit. But I'm no nearer making a decision. The problem is that if I go to the police now, they'll want to know why I didn't hand in the key straight away. Plus, they'll probably question me for hours about what she said in her dying moments. If I'd realised she'd put the key in my pocket, I'd have listened more carefully. I don't think I could go through all that again. More importantly, as no one else saw this mystery man, I'm not convinced that the inspector doesn't have me down as the main suspect.'

'Rubbish. If he thought that, he'd have taken you straight to the station. Your clothes would have been taken in evidence and you'd never have found the key.'

I let out a long sigh. 'Jewel of Happiness said to tell no one.'

'You've told me!'

'You don't count, but I'm not sure I trust Inspector Hamamoto.'

'Okay,' she said doubtfully. 'Didn't you said earlier she told you to take it to someone? Could she be talking about the key?'

I nodded. 'I think you're right. I seem to recall her saying something like, "Take it to White Tiger". None of it made any sense at the time, not least because I didn't realise she'd given me the key.'

'Could White Tiger be another code name?'

'I suppose so.'

'How are you meant to find this person, assuming it is a person?'

'She didn't say. The only place she mentioned was a shrine. Itsu… something or other.'

'Itsukushima?'

'Possibly. But I couldn't swear to it. Is it far? Can we get there?'

'It's in Hiroshima. Or rather, on an island not far from the city. It's the next stop on our itinerary.'

'But it will be days before we get there.'

'Which will give us plenty of time to work out how we

are going to find this White Tiger person when we get there.'

There was no time to discuss White Tiger or Water Dragon that evening. Aunt Jessica was due to give the second of her presentations at six o'clock and needed some time to look through her notes and get herself ready. After that, we all went out together for a meal.

We shared our table with the Bensons – Curtis and Isabel. They were a pleasant couple and neither of them made any reference to the events at the tea house. Not that I put them anywhere near the top of the list of possibilities when it came to identifying the real Fox in any case.

'Congratulations on another fascinating talk this evening, Jessica. I confess I hadn't even heard of Nara before we came here let alone that it was Japan's first capital city. It looks a fantastic place if those photos you showed us are anything to go by. I'm really looking forward to going there tomorrow.' Isabel's enthusiasm seemed quite genuine and not mere polite convention. 'Were they all your own photos?'

'Yes, but Harry's the one who put them all together.'

Curtis turned to me. 'I thought the way you zoomed in to see the details of the architecture Jessica was identifying was truly impressive. Really professional.'

'I don't know about that, but I can find my way round PowerPoint. That's the programme I used to put the slides together.'

'I'm familiar with PowerPoint, at least the basics, but I never realised you could do all those fancy animations and picture manipulation with it.'

'They aren't difficult. Fairly straightforward really. You don't need to be that technically expert.'

'Then you'll have to show me a few tricks sometime. I give quite a few talks myself to local groups back home.'

'Really? What's your subject?'

'Steam locomotives. It's been a hobby of mine since I was a kid. Now I'm retired, and have more time, I've written a couple of books about them.'

'How interesting,' I said trying to inject some enthusiasm into my voice though, in all honesty, I could think of few things more boring.

'I'd love to know how you add moving lines to maps like you did in tonight's talk.'

Curtis and I talked animation for a few minutes while Aunt Jessica and Isabel chatted about the day's trip.

'Last evening, Jessica mentioned something about you building her a website.'

'That's right. Technology has moved on quite a bit since her previous one. The thing is, although there are lots of designers out there who will create a flash looking website for you, it really is much better to do it yourself and then you can keep it updated. I'll admit, it takes a bit of time to get your head round the software, but it is worth the effort.'

'Easy for you to say,' Curtis said with a wry laugh. 'My publisher handles all the book production side of things, but he keeps telling me I need to get myself a website. I've looked at several of those companies who advertise web design, but apart from the fact they charge the earth, other authors in my position have said just what you did. If you are going to keep it relevant to your readers, you need to do it yourself so you can keep it updated. That's all very well, but for us oldies who grew up with pen and paper, all this technology malarkey is far from second nature like it is with you young people. I suppose you do a lot of this kind of thing in your work?'

I shook my head and smiled. 'Not really. I use computers obviously but not for design.'

'What line of work are you in?'

The dreaded question. 'To be honest I'm between jobs at the moment. I used to work in a bank, but I moved from Bedford to London a couple of months ago. I planned to take a bit of a break. I've been helping my aunt in the meantime as I said, but when we go return home, I'm not sure I want to go back to banking. I was in a rut and it's time for a change. A fresh challenge.'

'And what are you planning on doing?'

'I'm not sure. I've been so busy these last few weeks, I haven't given much thought to the future. I'll need to find something in the interim obviously, but I don't want to make any hasty decisions about the long term.'

'Well, if you've got time on your hands and you'd like to earn yourself a bit of cash while you look around for something permanent, do you think you could help develop a website for me? I've been looking at the things other writers are doing and I've a fair idea of what I want. I've even bought this software package designed specifically for authors, but I just can't seem to get my head round all the bells and whistles. I don't understand all the technical language they use like widgets and things I've never heard of.'

He looked at me expectantly and when I hesitated, he said.

'I'm not trying to put you on the spot. There's no need to give me an answer here and now. Just think about it and let me know. No pressure! But I'll make it worth your while.'

'And it would save me from hearing a great deal of bad language,' added Isabel wearing a pained expression.

'I smiled. 'I'll definitely think about it.'

CHAPTER 9

Neither of us said much as we made our way back to the hotel. The more I thought about it, the more attractive Curtis's offer seemed. At least the idea of earning some cash. There were lots of questions I'd need to ask him first, of course – where he lived for a start. The bulk of the work I could do at home, but we'd need several face-to-face meetings. If I had to travel up to Scotland or all the way to Cornwall, it would be a non-starter. Perhaps I could get him to come to me. And I'd need to have a look at this software he had. Still, no point in getting too excited. People say these things, especially on holiday, but he'd probably have forgotten all about it by the time we got back to the hotel.

It wasn't until we were in the lift that I realised Aunt Jessica had said nothing for the last quarter of an hour. I pressed the button for our floor and turned to look at her. She was staring into the distance chewing on her bottom lip.

I felt a tightening in my stomach. 'Penny for them.'

She shook her head, 'Just thinking.'

The doors slid open with a soft hiss and she marched down the corridor to her room, unlocked her door and stepped inside. I wasn't sure if she wanted me to follow but she held the door open until I joined her.

'Something wrong?' I asked as I hovered in the doorway.

For the first time, she looked directly at me. 'No, not at all. Come on in.' The smile was reassuring.

By the time I'd closed the door, she had thrown her

jacket on the bed and was retrieving her laptop from the safe.

'Sorry if I was a bit uncommunicative on the way back but I didn't want to say anything with other people around. I think it's about time we found out a bit more about these code names,' she said as she plugged in her machine and switched it on. 'Fix us both a nightcap while it warms up, sweetie.'

'What do you want to look up, exactly?'

'I don't think these names Jewel of Happiness mentioned are quite as random as they seem. It occurred to me earlier that they might have some significance in Japanese mythology.'

It was no easy task surfing through the possible sites but eventually we found mention of a fox. I perched on the end of the bed, trying not very successfully to read over her shoulder as she skimmed down the page.

'It says here that the Japanese word for fox is kitsune, but in mythology, the kitsune is a magical fox, a creature of immense wisdom and power. The more it grows in wisdom, the more tails it grows. Kitsune can have up to nine tails. Once they reach a hundred years of age, they gain the ability to shapeshift into a human form.'

'Can't see that helps very much.'

'Maybe not, but it goes on to say that they have become closely associated with a Shinto spirit and serve as its messengers. Bingo!'

'Messenger. That works. What about White Tiger?'

After looking at a few more sites, Aunt Jessica said, 'There's not a lot here. All I can find is a reference to White Tiger being one of the four symbols of the constellations. It represents the west.'

'Nothing about it being the keeper of secrets?'

'No, but...' She tapped away at the keyboard and brought up a map of Japan. 'As I thought, Hiroshima isn't quite on the most westerly point of Honshu, but it's a long way west of Kyoto and Itsukushima Shrine is on an island fifteen miles south west of the city.'

'Well, that sort of fits.'

'What was the other name? Water Dragon?'

'That was it.'

Finding any reference to a water dragon proved a laborious task. The only reference Aunt Jessica could find was to the Mizuchi, a legendary serpent-like creature, either found in an aquatic habitat or linked to water in some way. It could breathe out venom, poisoning and killing innocent passers-by. Given Jewel of Happiness's warning, the fact that it was dangerous was hardly a revelation.

It was gone midnight by the time I got to my own room and apart from having trouble actually getting to sleep, disturbing dreams involving hissing snakes and dragon heads appearing out of the mists snorting venomous smoke from its nostrils woke me with a start several times.

CHAPTER 10

It was an early start the next morning. We left the hotel at eight to catch a train to Nara, Japan's first permanent capital city.

'Wow! Not much like St Pancras, is it?'

Not only was the station spacious and spotlessly clean with plenty of comfortable seats, it had its own shopping mall and the food stalls were spectacular.

'This is probably the best place to get yourself a snack to have at lunch time,' Gerri told us. 'They do some tasty little food trays known as Bento boxes.'

She led us to a line of stalls filled with small card boxes divided into sections with an interesting assortment of titbits which, apart from rice and sushi rolls, I couldn't identify.

'I think I'd be happy going back to the stalls over there and buying myself a couple of pieces of fruit and one of those interesting looking cakes,' I said to Aunt Jessica.

'Where's your sense of adventure?'

'When it comes to food I don't recognise, I left it at home,' I said firmly.

Isabel was the last to return to the meeting point where Aiko, who would be with us until we returned to Kyoto, and Gerri were rounding us all up ready to take us to our platform.

'I still can't get used to Japanese toilets. Warm, soft padded seats just aren't my thing, but I'm terrified of all those buttons down the side in case I press the wrong one.'

'I take it you haven't tried either of the bidet sprays then?' Aunt Jessica said with a mischievous grin.

Isabel gave a mock shudder.

'The music accompaniment is nice though,' said Lucy. 'I read somewhere that's to stop the ladies feeling embarrassed at the noise of natural functions.'

Inevitably that led to all sorts of lively banter that turned into a few risqué jokes and I felt cheerful and light-hearted as we waited for the train. That was until I noticed Aunt Jessica taking a surreptitious look around at the people on the platform. If she recognised our stalkers, she didn't mention it, so I decided not to let it spoil my day by asking, and resolutely pushed the whole idea to the back of my mind.

The train journey was a great opportunity to study our fellow travellers. Some people you warm to straight away and there are others, for no good reason that you can explain, it's difficult to take to. In my case, Josh Rutherford was one of the latter. In theory, we had a fair amount in common – both single, around the same age and British – though he had the advantage of good looks and, from the quality of his clothes and the expensive watch he sported, he was not short of a bob or two. His sex appeal was not lost on Lucy. She never wasted an opportunity to be at his side. Time would tell if the attraction was mutual.

The journey to Nara passed without incident. Everyone seemed in an exceptionally good mood and the horrors of Wednesday's events at the tea house were not mentioned.

We walked from the station along the main road until we reached the park. There seemed to be more deer than people.

'You might like to buy some deer-crackers to feed them. These deer are very tame, and you'll find yourselves quickly surrounded by them waiting to be fed. If you hold out your biscuit, they will come up to you, but before they accept it, they will bow three times,' explained Aiko.

'Very Japanese,' said Chandler.

'Are you sure they don't bite?' Isabel sounded unsure.

Aiko gave her a beaming smile. 'They are very gentle, but you shouldn't tease them. These Nara sika deer are considered sacred to the gods in the Shinto religion and have been designated a national treasure.'

'There's certainly enough of them. How many are there?' asked Curtis.

'I believe the last count was around 1,500.'

As everyone was preoccupied asking questions, buying snacks or feeding the deer, Aunt Jessica slipped an arm through mine and gently steered me to where our conversation could not be overheard.

'Please refrain from doing what you did last time when I said, "Don't look now," and turn round, just keep looking at me. I think we are being watched again. There's a young man in jeans wearing a dark blue baseball cap who's been hanging around on the other side of the road for the last ten minutes. I'm fairly certain it's the same one we spotted at Nijo Castle. I think I saw him on the platform before we got on the train. He wasn't wearing the cap then, but his T-shirt's the same colour. He had more sense than to follow us from Nara station, but all the tourists come this way, so he'd have realised we'd be here.'

'Any sign of the other one?' I held out a biscuit to one of the deer, which immediately encouraged others. We were surrounded by animals in seconds.

'I haven't spotted him yet. If he is any good at his job, he's probably walked on up to the temple, discreetly hidden waiting for our arrival.'

We didn't have to wait until we reached the temple. Our older watcher, or at least an individual Aunt Jessica was ninety percent sure was the same man, was hanging around Nandaimon Gate, a huge wooden structure that marked the entrance to the temple complex.

As we climbed up the steps to pass through the first of the three great openings, a man stood staring up at the eight-metre-high wooden figure standing within an alcove in the gate's inner wall. Aunt Jessica glanced at me and raised an eyebrow.

'There is another guardian statue in the same spot on the other side of the gate which you might like to see before we move on. These monumental figures are known as the Two Kings of Tōdai-ji. Like the gate itself, they date back to the early thirteenth century…' As Aiko continued her spiel, I tried to position myself in the group to take a good look at our watcher without it appearing too obvious, but he hurried down the far steps making for the collection of stalls and disappeared into the crowd of tourists who were eagerly inspecting the souvenirs on offer.

'I wouldn't like to meet him on a dark night!'

It took a second or two to appreciate that Lucy was referring to the wide-eyed, teeth bearing face of the statue glaring down at us from above.

'He's there to scare off the evil demons,' said Josh who was standing beside her.

We were given fifteen minutes of free time to look around the gate and the stalls. I hung back with Aunt Jessica at the tail end of the group as we all dutifully trooped round to look at the second guardian.

'I didn't really have time to take a good look at our watcher before he scurried off,' I had to admit. 'And to be honest, I only got a glimpse of him at Nijo Castle. Do you really think it's the same man?'

'As certain as I can be.'

'So, what do we do about it?'

'I suggest when we all move off again, you stick like glue to the group for the rest of the trip. I'll hang back at some point and see what happens. If we're given any more time to wander on our own at any stage, latch on to someone and don't be alarmed or start looking around for me if I disappear. I want to see what happens. To spot the spotters.'

CHAPTER 11

The whole complex was a large area that included twenty or so buildings that belonged to the Buddhist monastery, which in its heyday must have housed a large number of monks. Hardly surprising given that Tōdai-ji was the head temple of all the provincial temples in Japan at a time when Buddhism was at its height. Entrance to the Great Buddha Hall at the heart of the complex was with a ticket so we all had to wait while Aiko went to buy them. Even after we joined the long line of eager visitors, it was obviously going to be a good ten minutes before we reached the middle gate. As we slowly shuffled forward, it was a good opportunity to look back casually and scan the crowds. I couldn't spot either of our stalkers.

Inside the great hall, I was so busy taking photos of the spectacular fifty-foot gold Buddha that I quickly forgot about everything else. I found myself rubbing shoulders with Bruce who was also a keen photographer.

'Difficult to find a spot to get the whole thing in, isn't it?'

I nodded in agreement. 'It is supposed to be the largest gilded statue in the world.'

We continued chatting and it was several minutes before I began to look around to see where Aunt Jessica had got to. I felt a moment of panic when she was nowhere in sight until I remembered her instruction.

I turned back to speak to Bruce. 'Molly will be wondering where you've got to.'

Bruce chuckled. 'I doubt it. She gets fed up waiting for me to finish taking photos especially as I tend to lag behind until everyone else has moved on. It's impossible to get shots without any people in the way, but I like to try.'

'I'm the same,' I said, doing my best to sound sympathetic. 'The trouble is as soon as one group of tourists moves off, another one jumps in and you're no better off.'

'That's a nice camera you've got there. Has it got one of the new eighteen to one forty lenses?'

'Erm…' I nodded.

I'm not quite sure why I didn't admit straight away that it wasn't my camera. Perhaps because he might start wondering why Aunt Jessica would part with it. I still hadn't decided if she'd told me to concentrate on taking lots of pictures while we were out to give her a chance to look out for our stalkers as she claimed, or in an attempt to keep me from brooding about the woman I nursed in my arms as she lay bleeding to death. Not to mention the possibility of being tailed by her killer.

Bruce was soon extolling the virtues of the lens he was planning on buying as soon as he could persuade his wife that it was worth the investment.

'Molly's not too keen. It is pricey and she's keen on us getting a new kitchen.'

Bruce and I left the temple and wandered towards the back of the complex to get pictures of some of the smaller buildings. It was more open in this section of the park and few people had ventured this far. This suited me fine as it meant that no one could sneak up on us without being spotted.

Once we got back from Nara, it was time to pack for our journey to Hiroshima. Our main cases would be taken north to Kanazawa and the third hotel on our trip, leaving us to carry only the things we needed for our two-night stay in Hiroshima. This would be my first experience travelling on one of the country's famous bullet trains and, like most of the others, I was looking forward to it.

At the station, Gerri led us along the platform to the white markers with the same number as the compartment shown on our tickets. We had to line up in twos behind the waist-high barrier at the edge of the platform.

'Those gates will open when the train stops. Don't waste any time getting on as the doors will close automatically after five minutes. Your seat number is printed on your ticket. We'll all be sitting in the same block, so I'll be there to answer any questions.'

'That's good,' Vincent said. 'You can tell us when to get off. Do we know what time we get there?'

'It's printed on your ticket,' Gerri answered. 'If it says we arrive at 18.17, that's when we get there. Not a minute either side.'

'That's Japanese precision for you,' said Josh.

The train arrived exactly on time and stopped at the point where the train doors lined up perfectly with the gap in the barrier once the gates drew back.

'The train's so quiet,' said Isabel, who was standing in front of me. She was excited as a small child.

There was little sense of speed as the train raced across southern Honshu towards our destination.

'I did expect to feel some sort of rolling motion. If you closed your eyes you wouldn't know you were on a moving vehicle,' I said to Aunt Jessica as I settled back into the comfortable seat and closed my eyes. I felt more relaxed than I had in days. 'I wondered if the inspector would allow me to leave Kyoto. I'm surprised he didn't come to the hotel to ask more questions. I wonder if the police have caught Jewel of Happiness's killer yet.'

'I don't think so,' Aunt Jessica said quietly.

'How do you know?'

'I asked the girl who cleans my room. She was at the end of the corridor when I came out this morning. She's trying to improve her English, so we stopped and chatted for several minutes. I asked her if there was any news. It seems to be a hot topic in the city. There are updates in the local media every day. There are lots of theories flying around.'

'Oh?' I was all attention.

'Most of the suggestions revolve around our geisha falling out with one of her clients. There's also talk that her death could be linked to the recent murder of the president of one of Japan's biggest banks and there's even rumours of the involvement of the yakuza.'

'You've lost me. What's yakuza?'

'It's the equivalent of the Japanese mafia.'

My stomach gave a sudden lurch. 'You mean someone powerful enough to send some of his minions to keep a tail on me in case she told me anything.'

'Possibly.'

'It must have been some secret she was keeping.'

Further discussion came to an abrupt stop as Gerri came round to check that everyone was happy and answer any questions we might have.

She was back again a little later with a large box of sweetmeats.

'You must try one of these. The Japanese don't use sugar, and these are made from sweet bean paste. It's a speciality.'

The large box contained a dozen or so pieces of disk-shaped confectionery an inch and a half or so in diameter and half an inch thick, separated by cardboard dividers. Tea flavoured bean paste didn't sound too appetising to me, plus they were a rather bilious shade of pale green and I was about to pass up on the proffered treat when Aunt Jessica gave me a sharp dig in the ribs.

'What happened to that promise you made last night about being more adventurous? You won't know unless you try it.'

Reluctantly, I took one, held it gingerly between my thumb and forefinger and stared at it. I tentatively nibbled the edge, then took a tiny bite.

'Actually, it's good.' I took a larger bite. 'Very good,' I

admitted and popped the whole thing in my mouth in one go. 'I could get quite addicted to these.'

Gerri smiled. 'You can see the locals cooking them on street stalls. That's when I like them best, while they're still warm. There are lots of different flavours and colours.'

After an hour or so, most people were either reading or dozing.

There had been no opportunity for Aunt Jessica and I to discuss what had happened at Nara. On the journey back to the hotel there'd been the risk of being overheard and once we got to the hotel, we only had time to collect our things ready to move on. Even now, though the higher seat backs in the bullet train afforded a little more privacy than this morning's local train, we still needed to be on our guard.

She changed the subject. 'Did you enjoy this morning?'

'Very much so,' I answered. 'Bruce is a nice guy.'

'I noticed you both went off taking photos. Did you get any good shots?'

'I'll show you when we get to the next hotel. We talked about cameras most of the time.'

'I see.'

'What about you? Did you enjoy your stroll? See anything particularly interesting?'

'Not really. I didn't like to get out of sight of the others. Most of our lot wandered out to the shops after a bit, but Josh and Lucy carried on to the back of the complex. They seemed to be taking a similar route to you and Bruce. Did they catch you up?' She gave me a pointed look.

'No. I didn't see them.' If Josh appeared to be keeping tabs on me, did that mean he was Fox? One way or another, nearly half the group had asked me in a roundabout way if Jewel of Happiness had said anything to me before she died, but Josh hadn't been one of them.

'Apart from the usual pleasantries, I don't think I've spoken much with Josh.'

I think Aunt Jessica understood what I was trying to say,

or rather not say, because she gave a smile and a nod.

'No, I'm not sure I have either. He was with Lucy and Joanna when we were talking about that poor geisha, but he didn't join in the conversation.'

'Couldn't get a word in, I expect,' I laughed. 'Those sisters can talk for England.'

So, even though he hadn't asked directly, he'd taken steps to be around when the questions were asked.

CHAPTER 12

Even when we reached our hotel in Hiroshima, Aunt Jessica and I still didn't have that much more time to talk. After we checked in, Gerri gave us half an hour to freshen up before leaving for dinner. It only took me ten minutes for a quick shower and make myself presentable. I waited another five minutes in case Aunt Jessica was still in the bathroom, then went to knock on her door.

It opened a little and her head poked round.

'Am I too soon? Are you ready?'

'Not quite, but you can come in.'

She opened the door wide and went back to her seat at the dressing table and began to brush her hair. Hers was the only chair so I parked myself on the bed. I let out a long sigh and lay back.

'For some reason, long journeys always make me tired. I'm shattered.'

She made sympathetic noises but didn't bother to turn and look at me.

'Do I take it that Tweedledum and Tweedledee didn't follow us into the temple this morning?' I hadn't meant to bring up the subject at all, but the whole situation was constantly in the back of my mind.

'I expect they were both there, but I only spotted the younger one. He stayed tucked amongst the crowd. The only reason I spotted him was because he kept glancing to see where you were. He seemed to get a bit agitated when you and Bruce wandered behind the temple by yourselves, presumably because he realised you might spot him if he tried to follow. He made a call on his mobile, pushed himself out of the group of people he was hiding in and made his way pretty smartly across to the other side of the temple building, presumably hoping to pick you up when you came out into view again.'

'I wonder if they've followed us to Hiroshima. Did you see them on the train?'

She put down the hairbrush and twisted round to face me, resting her arms on the back of the chair. 'No, but there were dozens of carriages. Those bullet trains are always very long. I doubt they needed to keep close anyway. They are not stupid. They will have a copy of our itinerary.'

I raised an eyebrow.

'Anyone can download it from the company website,' she said dismissively. 'I think it's fair to say that they don't have any plans to kidnap you.'

'Well that's some consolation, I suppose, but what makes you so sure?'

'Because they would have done it by now,' she said impatiently. 'It's pretty obvious that what they are after is to see who you make contact with. You are not likely to do that while we're travelling. Any handover is much more likely to take place on one of the tours. Though I've no doubt someone will be keeping a watch to see if you slip out of the hotel at any point.'

'I wonder if they know I have the key.'

'Possibly.' She gave a slight frown and sat upright, a faraway look in her eyes.

After a moment or two of silence, I said, 'What are you thinking?'

She looked at me again, pushed herself up from the chair and came to sit next to me on the bed.

'In all of this, we haven't given much thought as to why Jewel of Happiness was so desperate to give you the key and tell you to take it to someone. What does that key open and how did she get hold of it? I was thinking while I was on the train. A couple of years ago, I was asked to give a lecture at a conference. It was about the place of women in ancient societies. Anyway, one of the speakers read her paper on the secret world of the geisha. She stressed how nothing that was said at the meetings between the geisha and her client was ever passed on. I remember she compared the geisha to a catholic priest in the confessional.'

'You think Jewel of Happiness learnt something that was so explosive, she decided to break that seal of trust?'

'It's certainly a possibility.'

'Her client got wind that she was intending to pass on that highly sensitive information and sent someone to kill her.'

'Whether he intended to kill her or simply threaten her we'll probably never know. You suddenly appearing on the scene may have necessitated a change of plans. We can be fairly certain that someone knew that Jewel of Happiness had something, be that a key or some highly sensitive information, she was going to pass on. I think there is a good chance that someone was sent to retrieve it before the handover could take place.'

'Which means, I'm now the one in danger.'

She shook her head. 'It's been three days since her murder. If that were true, at the very least, your room would have been ransacked or you'd have been waylaid and threatened until you'd handed over what Jewel of Happiness had given you. I think she must have told her killer he was too late. That the information had already been passed on.'

'So why are they following me?'

'We can only assume that she never told them where that information now is. Which means they still haven't recovered it. They are following you in the hope that you might lead them to it. I wanted to hang back this morning not only to try and spot those two but to see if any of our party showed any interest in what you were up to.'

'The real Fox, you mean?' She nodded.

'On the train, you hinted that it might be Josh.'

'He and Lucy were taking photos of the side of the temple and they walked to the back. Then they returned the same way rather than follow you and Bruce.'

'Do you think they were checking to see if there was anyone else back there that I'd gone to contact.'

'I think that's not an unreasonable assumption, but it could be perfectly innocent. Let's not rule out any of the rest just yet.' She glanced at her watch and stood up. 'But right now, I think it's time for us to join the others.'

The next morning, our new local guide for Hiroshima was waiting for us with Gerri in the hotel lobby. I'm not the world's best person at judging people's ages and add oriental features to the mix and all I will claim is that Haruto was a young man, possibly around my age. Our previous guide had mentioned her teenaged son and a married daughter expecting her first baby. I realised that my assessment that she was in her late twenties or early thirties was way off the mark. But, in my defence, when she talked about her children's ages, everyone else in the party was as surprised as I was.

Haruto appeared far more staid and serious than Aiko. He was even dressed as though about to go to the office. No tie, but a black button-to-the-neck jacket with a mandarin collar. He made a formal bow to us all when Gerri introduced him, and his voice was high and squeaky.

'He's going to be a barrel of laughs,' came a low whisper from Vincent who was standing behind me.

I tried to stop the giggle threatening to erupt by turning it into a cough. Behind my hand, I whispered back, 'My thoughts exactly.'

'This morning, we will be taking a short tram ride to the edge of the Seto Sea. There we will board the ferry for a short passage across to Miajima Island. This tranquil island is the home to Itsukushima Shrine. The red Torii Gate that sits in the waters is one of the most photographed sites in Japan.'

He sounded as though he was reading a script from some travel guide. 'In ancient times, access to holy Miyajima Island was through this floating gate.'

We all trooped out of the hotel behind Haruto, leaving Gerri to bring up the rear.

'The only consolation is that we only have him for the one day. Tomorrow we'll be off again,' Aunt Jessica said once we were outside.

The journey to the shrine was uneventful. If the two men who had kept a watch on us in Kyoto were also in Hiroshima they weren't in evidence.

'Do you think they've given up?' I asked Aunt Jessica once we'd boarded the ferry and had moved out of earshot from the rest of our party.

'Perhaps their employer already had contacts here in Hiroshima.'

'I suppose that means we have two new goons to identify in all the crowds,' I said bitterly.

Aunt Jessica patted me on the shoulder. 'Take comfort in the fact that if the plan was to silence you in any way, they'd have done so long before now.'

'So you keep telling me.'

'Have you thought any more about how you are going to find White Tiger?'

We had discussed this problem when we'd come back to the hotel last night. Not that either of us had come up with any ideas.

'I've been thinking about little else all morning. I'm just keeping my fingers crossed that he will find me.'

'Then we'll just have to play it by ear.'

'Once I've passed on this wretched key, I hope my stalkers will realise there is no point following me anymore.'

'Let's hope so. By the way, have you noticed our two love birds appear to have had a falling out?'

Her attempt to change the subject met with a grunt from me. I could see Lucy and her sister laughing together in the rear of the ferry and I looked around for Josh. He was at the front all on his own peering across the water with his binoculars?

'You could be right,' I conceded. 'But just because they aren't side by side doesn't mean they've fallen out.'

'True, but I noticed they've been giving each other a wide berth all morning.'

CHAPTER 13

The ferry glided slowly on its final approach into the terminal. We disembarked and Gerri and Haruto gathered us up and led us past the cafes and shops lining the path to the shrine. Not that we took much notice of the shops. All eyes were on the magnificent floating torii gate, one of the most recognised sites in Japan and a landmark that had become a national symbol for the country. I was overawed by the sheer grandeur of the spectacle. I still had my aunt's camera, and this was an opportunity not to be missed. The sun was shining, and I was so preoccupied trying to work out which was the best spot from which to get the perfect photograph of the gate reflected in the water that I momentarily forgot my troubles.

To give him his due, as we got closer, our guide Haruto realised that there was little point in trying to round us up until we'd all had a chance to take more pictures. Either that or Gerri had had a quiet word with him.

Some ten minutes later, we stood listening to Haruto's account of the 1,400 years of history of the shrine. He wittered on about how it was established by some empress and then gave us a whole list of warriors whose names washed straight over my head, each of whom added more buildings in celebration of their victories. Haruto may have known his stuff, but I suspect that the others were getting as impatient as I was, waiting for him to shut up and let us move on and go across to the shrine itself.

The shrine turned out to be not a single building, but a collection of temples constructed in the water and all linked by an open-sided corridor with its beautifully carved roof held up by red-painted wooden pillars. We passed the first few small temples and other buildings and came out onto an open area in the centre of the complex.

Across the water outside the first temple, a wedding party were gathering for the official photographs. It was a traditional wedding. The bride and all the female guests were dressed in richly embroidered kimonos, and the groom was sporting a mauve tunic and a most unusually shaped hat held on with white ribbon around his neck. The two fathers seated on the front row on either side of the bride and groom in the centre, were also in traditional garb albeit in sober short black kimono type jackets and dark grey skirts.

It was only when the official photographer had finished, and the wedding party got to their feet and turned to go that Haruto was able to persuade us all to move on. I stood looking at the shots I'd managed to get when I felt a gentle hand on my arm.

'I managed to get some brilliant pictures with your camera. Look at this…'

Aunt Jessica ignored my chatter and said quietly, 'Do you see what I see?'

I looked where she was indicating back across the water at the wedding party now retreating into one of the buildings. At first, I couldn't work out what she was talking about, then I saw it. One of the women who had been standing on the back row had a huge white tiger motif embroidered on the back of her lemon-coloured kimono.

My first thought was to race back through the maze of corridors to catch her but, looking back at the end of the platform area, I realised how futile my efforts would be. It was a one-way system and the passageways were crowded with people. There was an official standing at the entrance marshalling people through, and from the look on his face, I doubted he'd let me go back in any case.

Aunt Jessica must have read my thoughts. 'I doubt it would be a good idea to leave the group anyway. We don't want to arouse suspicion. There are too many people around and one of our stalkers could well be hidden in the crowd.'

I nodded and we both joined the rest of the group strung out behind Haruto. I tried to console myself with the thought that there was a strong possibility that the wedding party who had returned to one of the buildings were going back for another part of the ceremony or more likely, some kind of wedding feast. I could hardly gate-crash. It couldn't be much longer before we were given free time anyway. Perhaps I could catch her when the celebrations were over.

I can't say I paid too much attention to Haruto's monotonous commentary for the rest of the tour. The final section seemed endless, but I seemed to recall Haruto saying something about there being 280 metres of corridor spanning the water linking some twenty or so different buildings. Finding White Tiger didn't look like being an easy proposition.

We came out of the shrine complex at the opposite side from where we'd come in.

'The rest of the morning is yours,' announced our guide. 'There is still much to see. Once you cross the bridge, off to the right you will find the Museum of History and Folklore of the island, the Aquarium and some shops, or you can turn left and up into the valley into Momijidani Park where you will see deer and large koi goldfish in the ponds. The cherry blossom is at its best right now and there are many walks. You may well see several more bridal couples posing for photographs especially on the red wooden bridges as you wander through the gardens. This is a very popular spot to come to have photographs taken even if the actual ceremony did not take place at the shrine itself. In Japan it is quite common to see newly married couples in public parks or places such as this. They come without their guests but dressed in their wedding clothes to have photographs taken several days after the marriage day itself.'

Most of the group set off to cross the steep hump-backed bridge. I turned to make my way round the back of the temple complex towards the entrance.

'Stop!' Aunt Jessica's voice was low but sharp. She put a hand on my arm.

'I have to get back to the entrance,' I hissed, pulling away from her. 'I need to find the wedding party.'

Her hand gripped more tightly. So tight, it was hurting my arm.

Aunt Jessica shook her head. 'And what then? Even if they are all still in there, we couldn't exactly barge in and with all those tourists passing through, waiting outside in the corridor would only draw attention. She must know our party would be here today, so we have to hope that she will find us.'

'But...'

'Sweetie, whoever set up this elaborate plan for Jewel of Happiness to pass on a key would not have left things to chance. This has all been planned with meticulous precision. It can't be mere coincidence that a woman with a white tiger embroidered on her kimono just happens to be here at the shrine on the very day our tour group is booked to visit the place.'

My aunt's assessment made sense. 'I suppose so.'

'The best thing we can do now is exactly what all the other tourists are doing once they've been round the shrine itself, and that is walk up the valley into the gardens. That's where she will be expecting the messenger to be.'

'But how will she find me?' I looked around wildly feeling a rising panic. 'She doesn't know who Fox is. I don't have nine tails.'

'No,' snapped Aunt Jessica. 'Kitsune only grow more tails with wisdom and you're showing precious little of that right now.'

'But *I'm* not the real Fox. How is she going to know I'm the one with the key?' I could hear my voice getting higher and higher. 'She might not even *be* White Tiger. For all we know, she might be an ordinary wedding guest who just happened to have a tiger embroidered on the back of her kimono.'

'Pull yourself together, Harry! The last thing we need right now is you having a hissy fit and drawing attention to yourself. Let's start walking.'

She tucked her arm in mine and I had no choice but to follow the last of the now fast disappearing members of our party. She had a point. I had let the tension get to me.

The high barrel bridge rose steeply. Most people were having to haul themselves up using the wooden rails. Climbing over it was a challenge and took all our concentration. On the far side, the path divided.

'Which way now?'

Aunt Jessica shrugged her shoulders. 'You choose.'

'Let's go to the park.'

As we climbed the path rising up into the valley I said, 'Do you think someone is following us again?'

'That's more than likely, which is why you need to do nothing to draw attention to yourself. Behave like all the other tourists. How about you take a few photos?'

There were some pretty views on either side and after a couple of shots, I took a few looking back down the valley. At least, that's what I was hoping anyone watching us would think. Rather than general wide-angled views of the shrine buildings in the distance, I focussed on the people strolling up behind us. The crowds had thinned considerably but there were still twenty or so tourists ambling up behind us. Even through the telescopic feature on the camera, I didn't see anyone acting suspiciously, but at least I could compare the photos with ones I taken earlier and any others I took later in the day.

A short while after, the path forked again. Off to the right we saw a bride and groom posing on one of the small attractive red wooden bridges. Although, unlike the couple we'd seen earlier, they were not in Buddhist Japanese traditional dress, she was wearing a stunning white kimono embroidered in gold thread and flowers in her hair typical for a Shinto wedding, and he was in a short black jacket and grey striped skirt similar to the those worn by the fathers at the first wedding. Like them, he sported a large white pompom at his waist.

'That red parasol he's holding is for good luck,' Aunt Jessica said.

I took photos from every angle from the other path. For a good ten minutes, I was so engrossed that all thoughts of finding White Tiger receded. In the days when I was living in Bedford, before I had to sell all my photography equipment, I'd belonged to the local photography society. There were regular competitions and, though I never achieved the Photographer of the Year award, I usually managed a couple of firsts, several second places and a good few highly commended by the end of the season. If I'd still been a member of the club, I was certain I'd have at least one prize-winning photo.

Aunt Jessica was patient. In her work on archaeological sites and in her more recent travel writing, she knew the importance of finding that perfect shot, but we weren't there to play tourist. A gentle cough brought me back to our mission.

'Shall we go on?' I asked.

'Given that no one has passed by in the last quarter of an hour, I wonder if we should go back and try another path.'

'If we do see White Tiger, what do we do? I can't exactly waltz up to her and say, "Are you White Tiger because Jewel of Happiness gave me this key to give you?" Now, can I?'

Aunt Jessica smiled. 'Definitely not. Apart from anything else, we'll have no idea of who's watching. I suggest I go up, admire her kimono and ask if I could have my picture taken with her. It's the sort of thing other tourists do. If you remember, everyone was doing it in Kyoto in the gardens of the Nijo Castle. I could perhaps put out a few feelers before we could swap places. You could pass the key over while I take a photo of you standing with her.'

'Great idea. All we have to do now is find her.'

CHAPTER 14

I put down my coffee cup and let out a great sigh.

'Well that was all a waste of time. What do we do now?'

We were sitting at a table by the window in one of the cafés on the main street that spread along the shoreline between the shrine and the ferry.

We'd spent the best part of an hour wandering around the park and the various temples and the museum but seen no sign of White Tiger.

Aunt Jessica gave no reply, but then I hadn't expected her to. I took a bite of what passed for a Japanese sandwich.

A sudden wail of sirens made everyone stop what they were doing and stare out of the window. Four police cars raced passed in quick succession, horns blaring, scattering the tourists out of the way.

Aunt Jessica and I looked at each other. The same thought had obviously struck us both. Something had happened to White Tiger.

She raised an eyebrow. I answered the unspoken question with a nod. I threw back the rest of my coffee in a single gulp and got to my feet. My hand hovered over the unfinished sandwich, decided against taking it, and rushed after Aunt Jessica who was already halfway to the door.

The police cars were parked at the end of the drivable road at the rear of the shrine. There was no sign of the policemen, but a small gathering of people was standing around the cars.

'Do you know what's going on?' Aunt Jessica asked a couple.

'All we know is that we were planning on going up into the park, but we got sent back. Two policemen were tying tape across the path stopping anyone going any further.'

'It looked as though other tourists already up there were being sent back as well,' his wife added.

The rumours were rife. One story was that several people had been shot, another that someone had been stabbed and an unlikely suggestion that a madman with an axe was running through the park attacking people at random. Theories as who the victim or victims might be were equally varied and untrustworthy.

'We should go,' said Aunt Jessica. 'The group are supposed to be meeting by the ferry in ten minutes.'

I nodded. It was obvious we'd learn nothing here for some time, if at all.

We were only a few minutes late, but it looked as though we were not the last. The others were standing around in small groups. From the excited chatter, news that something dramatic was happening in the park had obviously reached them.

Ten minutes later, several people were still missing. Haruto was getting agitated, the first emotion I notice him show all day, but Gerri was calm enough.

'We will miss our ferry,' I heard him protest.

Gerri merely shrugged her shoulders. 'Then we'll catch the next one.'

'But our driver will be expecting us.'

'Then he'll have to wait. He's not going to drive off without us.'

I looked around to see who we were still waiting for. I couldn't see Josh Rutherford or the two Parkes sisters.

'Do you think the three of them are together?' asked Isabel.

No one seemed to know.

Gerri asked, 'Did anyone see where they were heading

after we left the shrine?'

More shaking heads.

'Here come the girls now,' someone called out.

We all turned to see. Amongst the steady stream of people making their way to the ferry, I could just make out the heads of the two sisters. As they got closer, it was clear Joanna had a protective arm around Lucy who appeared to be nursing a heavily bandaged forearm. They were making slow progress as Lucy was limping.

'Are you okay?' Gerri hurried towards them.

'I'm so sorry,' Lucy said. 'I tripped and fell. My arm was bleeding, so I had to go into a chemist and get it bandaged up.'

'Come and sit down.' Gerri guided her over to a convenient bench. 'What about your leg?'

'I twisted my ankle, that's all. It's nothing serious, but it still hurts a bit when I put weight on it.'

As everyone fussed over Lucy, Gerri turned to look back along the road. 'There's still no sign of Josh. I take it he wasn't with you two?'

Joanna shook her head.

We waited for another fifteen minutes.

'Do you think something has happened to him?' asked Gail. 'Perhaps he's fallen like Lucy. Shouldn't someone go and look for him?'

Chandler gave a derisive snort. 'Considering no one has any idea where he was headed, he could be anywhere. That whole area up into the park is vast.'

Gerri took Haruto aside. I tried to listen in to what they were saying but it was all in Japanese. After a couple of minutes, Gerri called us all back together.

'As you all realise, we have a bit of a problem. We've decided that Haruto will take you all back to Hiroshima and continue with the day's planned programme. I'm going to wait here and try to find out what has happened to Josh. The two of us will join you all later.'

'But what if you don't…'

Gerri cut in before Molly had time to frame the obvious question, 'The ferry will be leaving in five minutes, so I need you all to follow Haruto now, otherwise you'll miss it.'

As everyone began to move off, Gerri took Aunt Jessica aside. 'Would you mind awfully, keeping an eye on Haruto for me? He is a bit anxious. Make sure he doesn't skimp on any of the itinerary or not give you all enough time in the museum. I know that means we'll be back to the hotel half an hour later than originally planned, but that will still give plenty of time before your talk this evening. And it's not as though we have a specific restaurant booking for tonight for dinner.'

'No problem.' Aunt Jessica patted Gerri's arm. 'Good luck. It'll all sort itself out, I'm sure.'

Gerri didn't look too certain. 'I have temporarily lost people before but there wasn't a madman on the loose then.'

It was only a short ferry ride back to the mainland. Lucy looked pale and accepted her sister's arm as we made our way to the waiting minibus. I felt pretty shaky myself. I would've dearly loved to talk with Aunt Jessica, but there wasn't much chance of that in the immediate future.

'The Hiroshima Peace Memorial Park and museum are dedicated to the memory of the 140,000 victims of the world's first nuclear attack that took place here on August 6th in 1945.'

The last place I wanted to visit was a museum which set out details of what happened when the atomic bomb was dropped on the city. I felt low enough as it was without an extra dose of misery.

After Haruto gave us a brief introduction, we were given time to look round on our own. The place was crowded. It wasn't only tourists who were visiting in their droves. A good many of the visitors were Japanese. Because it was a Sunday, we were at least spared from the hordes of school children who are brought to learn about a significant day in the history not just of the country but the whole world.

There were so many people that I quickly lost sight of Aunt Jessica. We'd entered the first hall together, but I turned to look at one of the displays and read the information. She'd disappeared by the time I'd finished without me realising. I spotted her with Lucy and Joanna a little while later. I thought about joining them, but decided Lucy still looked a bit pale after her fall and probably needed a bit of mothering.

When it came time for the group to meet up again, Aunt Jessica was still with the two girls. They were all sitting on a bench. I wandered over and caught the tail end of their conversation.

'Are you sure? There is a lot of walking.' Joanna had a worried frown.

'My ankle is much better now, and my arm was only grazed. I'll admit it bled a lot, but it wasn't a deep cut and the pharmacist cleaned it for me.'

'But you were badly shaken,' Joanna insisted.

'I can easily call a taxi and get you back to the hotel,' Aunt Jessica suggested.

'Good idea. I'll come with you,' Joanna said quickly before Lucy had a chance to reply.

'I don't want to cause a fuss. I'll just sit here and wait until you all get back.'

'I believe we're going to be picked up at the end of the park by the atomic dome over there.' Aunt Jessica pointed to a large structure at the far end of the park.

'That does look quite some distance,' Lucy admitted.

'Then you and I are going back right now.' Joanna's tone brooked no refusal.

'I'll be fine on my own. There's no need for you to miss anything.'

As everyone else began to gather, Haruto was busy on his mobile. I wondered at first if he was phoning for a taxi for Lucy, but the way he was jabbering away for some time suggested otherwise.

When he finished his call, he clapped his hands for

attention. 'I have just spoken to Miss Hardy and she has found the missing member of your party.'

There were cheers all round and cries of, 'Thank goodness,' 'Great news,' and similar comments.

'Did Gerri say what happened to him?'

'Only that he is unharmed, and they will be returning to the hotel. Which means we should now continue with our tour.'

Aunt Jessica insisted that he should wait until the taxi had arrived for Lucy and Joanna. He looked none too pleased, but Aunt Jessica can be formidable when she sets her mind to it.

As it happened, we didn't have long to wait as there was a taxi rank just the other side of the museum.

CHAPTER 15

All sorts of questions filled my mind as we trailed in Haruto's wake, but there was little point in getting myself into a spin speculating on all the possibilities. I clutched at the comfort blanket Aunt Jessica had given me – her camera – and did my best to concentrate on the rest of the tour.

Our first stop was not far into the park at a tall futuristic three-legged structure surmounted by a young girl holding aloft the frame of a giant bird of some sort.

'This is the monument to all the children who died in the disaster. The girl on the top is Sadako Sasaki, who died of leukaemia caused by radiation poisoning. Before she died, she wanted to fold a thousand paper cranes. Japanese tradition says that if someone creates a thousand origami cranes, they are granted one wish. Sadako's wish was to have a world without nuclear weapons. As you can see thousands of cranes from all over the world have been brought here.'

He pointed to the semi-circle of glass cabins behind us each one containing a colourful display of what looked like streamers hanging down from hooks on the roof of an open-work metal frame.

'If you look closely,' he continued, 'you can see, each of the strings is made up of paper cranes. In Japanese culture, the cranes also carry souls up to paradise. The paper crane is the most classic of all Japanese origami.'

He opened his satchel and began handing out a small paper crane to each of us. As everyone wandered over to inspect the streamers, I sidled round to Aunt Jessica's side.

'I wonder what happened to Josh?' It wasn't the question I really wanted to ask, which was if she thought he could be the real Fox. It didn't seem a good idea to come out with it in public, though I doubted if any of the others could overhear us.

'Pointless to start guessing,' she said more sharply than I would have wished. 'Besides, we'll find out soon when we get back to the hotel.'

But, I thought, he's hardly likely to tell us if he is Fox.

Despite the half-hour delay leaving Itsukushima Shrine, we arrived back at the hotel with plenty of time to spare before the evening's lecture. Needless to say, there was no sign of Josh, but I had thought Gerri would be waiting for us in the lobby if only to come out to say goodbye and thank you to Haruto. I wasn't the only one who was disappointed. The rest of the party were equally curious as to what had happened to Josh.

'We'll just have to wait till Jessica's lecture,' said Vincent.

'Assuming Josh turns up.' Gail's expression indicated that she didn't think that was a likely proposition.

'In which case, you will have to curb your nosiness and wait until we all go out for dinner.' Before his wife could make any reply, Vincent laced his arm through hers and steered her to the lift.

I knew Aunt Jessica liked time to herself to look through her lecture beforehand, but there was no way I could wait until after our evening meal before getting her take on what had been happening. I knocked on her door ten minutes later.

Her expression wasn't stony, but it wasn't exactly welcoming either.

Before she could turn me away, I said quickly, 'Just five minutes?'

She pulled the door open and turned back into her room. I followed her down the short passageway by the bathroom and we both sat on the bed.

'Any more news?' I asked hopefully.

'No. Not yet.'

'There are so many questions running round my head. Who was attacked? Could it have been White Tiger? Was Josh late because he was lost or caught up in the attack? Did he go looking for her? Was that because he is the real Fox or because he's on the other side, possibly the one who attacked her?'

'Right now, there is no way we have any information that would help us answer any of those questions.'

'But what do you think?' I pleaded.

She shook her head. 'Why should my guesses be any better than yours?'

'Because you've been involved in all sorts of investigations in the past.'

'What on earth makes you think that?'

It had slipped out without me realising. My mother had always said that I was a dreamer and Aunt Maud claimed I lived in a fantasy world. To some degree, I suppose it was inevitable. There were few boys of my own age in the village and I was always a bit of a loner at secondary school in Norwich. Life in the Hamilton household was no better. My other aunts never missed a chance to show their disappointment in me. Aunt Jessica was the only one who seemed to understand me, but she was a rare visitor in the claustrophobic world of my youth. She spent her life in exotic places. Although I knew she was an archaeologist, which occasionally brought her into conflict with smugglers and graverobbers and the like, I had this vision of her working undercover for MI6 trying to foil some dastardly plot. Why that childish conviction should surface now, I had no idea.

'The aunts mentioned something about you being in dangerous situations when you were excavating digs,' I said weakly.

'Did they, now?'

I noticed she didn't deny it.

'And the last thing Mum said to me as I left the house was not to let you get me into trouble,' I added with what I hoped was a disarming smile. She also said that her older sister attracted trouble like honey attracts bees, but I decided not to mention that.

Aunt Jessica laughed. 'No sense of adventure, that's the trouble with my sisters. Anyway, for what it's worth, I'll give you my two pennyworth. I think it's too much of a coincidence that there was an attack at the shrine on the day we were visiting. But exactly who was attacked, we will just have to wait to find out.' She shrugged her shoulders.

'Or perhaps he's Water Dragon's agent and the one who killed White Tiger.'

Aunt Jessica stared into the distance for a few seconds then shook her head. 'I'll grant you he did manage to shake off Lucy this morning, but I seriously doubt he was the one who attacked White Tiger.'

'Why?'

'The plan for Jewel of Happiness to pass on a key to White Tiger via an intermediary was obviously set up well in advance. I think that whoever is out to stop that happening is reacting to the situation. Otherwise, why didn't they kill Jewel of Happiness before she arrived at the tea house? I can't believe they had time to get someone on the tour as backup just in case their plan failed.'

I nodded, 'I suppose so.'

She got to her feet. 'Now, I really need some time to get ready.'

At the door, I turned back with one last question. 'I don't suppose you spotted our watchers today?'

It was several seconds before she answered. 'I can't be certain, but possibly. Someone sitting in a café window as we walked up to the shrine after we got off the ferry seemed very interested in our group and I spotted the same man a couple of times after that in the shrine. He had a camera but seemed more interested in us than in taking photos.'

My heart gave a jump. 'Why didn't you mention it when we were there?'

'I kept checking but there was no sign of him in the park, so I was probably mistaken. No point in worrying you.'

I closed the door and went back to my room. I may not have been worried then, but sure as hell, I was now.

Everyone was pleased to see Josh when he came into the small conference room for Aunt Jessica's talk. The questions came thick and fast.

'What happened to you?'

'Did you get lost?'

'Are you alright?'

He put up his hands as though to ward off the attention.

'Let's all sit down, shall we.' Aunt Jessica's voice rose above the hubbub.

When order was restored, all eyes turned expectantly to Josh.

'The police wanted to talk to me, which is why I didn't get back in time. I was within the area they cordoned off. I wasn't close to the actual spot the woman was attacked so I was one of the last people to be interviewed.'

'Do you know what happened?'

'I was making my way up to one of the buildings in the park when half a dozen policemen ran past me. I went to see what was happening. There must have been twenty or so people already there and two of the policemen were already pushing everyone back and putting out do-not-cross tape. From what I could gather, a woman had been attacked. Her throat had been cut.'

Isabel gave a small cry and put her hands to her mouth.

'So, if you didn't see what happened, why did the police want to talk to you?' asked Chandler.

'They wanted to know if I'd seen anyone running away or acting suspiciously.'

'And did you?' Chandler persisted.

'Well I certainly didn't see anyone covered in blood or

wielding a blood-stained axe or whatever, if that's what you mean,' Josh joked. 'But I suppose that's why the police put a cordon round that whole section of the park – searching for the murder weapon.'

CHAPTER 16

Aunt Jessica hardly spoke as we all made our way to dinner after her talk. Like me, her mind was probably in overdrive. I wasn't in the mood to study every restaurant window before making a decision about my choice of dish. Apart from anything else, despite having no more than a couple of bites of the sandwich I'd chosen at lunch, I didn't feel hungry anyway. Aunt Jessica and I went into the first restaurant we came to.

The place was already filling rapidly with only three or four empty tables left. We settled ourselves at one towards the back of the room. Any hopes for a private chat were dashed when Curtis and Isabel entered the restaurant and, seeing us, made their way to our table.

'May we join you?' Curtis asked.

'Of course.' Aunt Jessica gave him a welcoming smile.

Any initial annoyance with them for thwarting my plans quickly dissipated. More so than with any of the others on the tour, I felt at ease with Curtis and Isabel. Curtis struck me as eminently sensible and easy to talk to, and Isabel was the motherly type. She was a bit of a fusser, but kind-hearted to a fault.

Though we talked about the morning's trip to Itsukushima Shrine, neither of them made any reference to the attack. Though it was probably uppermost in all our minds, it was as though by some unspoken agreement everyone had decided not to let the shocking event intrude on the evening. That was another reason to like this friendly couple. They never gave way to indulging in sensational gossip for the sake of it like so many.

'I loved seeing the wedding party in all their finery,' enthused Isabel. 'Did you see the beautiful kimonos the mothers were wearing?'

She and Aunt Jessica were soon talking wedding finery. Curtis looked at me across the table with a shake of the head. 'What is it about women and weddings?'

I returned his conspiratorial grin.

'Have you thought any more about helping me with my website?' he asked quietly as the women chatted on.

'I'll need to have a better idea of what you want before committing myself, but I am interested.'

'Naturally. Perhaps we can get together tomorrow and discuss it. Is Jessica giving another talk in the evening?'

'Yes, but I can't see that being a problem.'

'That sounds fine. Tomorrow it is then. Let's fix the time and place when we arrive at the next hotel.'

The four of us strolled back together to the hotel.

'Fancy a snifter in the bar?' asked Curtis as we walked into the lobby.

It would have been rude to refuse. As I sank down into one of the padded bucket seats in the small bar, I decided that until we had more information about the identity of the victim at Itsukushima, I might as well push it all to the back of my mind and enjoy the evening in good company.

'So, what's everyone having?'

As Curtis disappeared to the bar with our orders, Isabel said, 'There aren't many people in here this evening. I expected to see some of our party.'

The only other drinkers were a couple of Japanese businessmen in the far corner.

'I expect they will turn up later. I think we must be among the first to get back.'

Curtis returned almost straight away. 'The barman said

he'd bring the drinks over.'

'What did you think of the visit to the Peace Park and the museum?' asked Isabel.

'I can't say I enjoyed it,' I replied carefully choosing my words, 'but I'm glad I went.'

'I thought it was pretty harrowing,' she said, giving a little shiver. 'Seeing all those children's clothes laid out and that sad little tricycle burnt to twisted metal.'

'The best you can say about it is that at least the atomic bomb forced Japan to concede and bring the war to an end,' said Curtis.

'Actually, it didn't. It's one of the myths the politicians of the time liked to put forward to justify the decision to bomb Hiroshima and Nagasaki.' Everyone looked at Aunt Jessica. 'The truth is that Japan had already decided to capitulate when Russia, who up until that point had been a neutral observer of the war in the east, decided to enter the fray and moved into China. By then, Japan had insufficient reserves of men and arms to fight one major enemy and knew that it stood no chance against two superpowers.'

The barman arrived with our drinks. 'Two white wines for ladies and two local beers for gentlemen.'

He placed them on the table and stood back giving a small bow.

'Thank you, young man.' Curtis looked up at him and smiled. 'Not many people in here tonight. Is it usually this empty?'

'Sunday evenings always less busy. Not so many businessmen at weekend. Only tourists. Two large parties move on this morning so tonight more quiet.'

'We are leaving first thing tomorrow as well,' said Isabel.

'You enjoy Hiroshima?'

'Very much,' we assured him.

'What you see? Go Peace Park? Very sad.'

'True, but Miyajima Island and Itsukushima Shrine were beautiful.'

A frown creased his forehead. 'In news tonight, it say

lady die. Attacked by man with knife.'

'They say bad news travels fast,' muttered Curtis.

'Did it mention if the police have caught the killer?' Aunt Jessica asked.

'No. He escape. Police asking for witnesses.'

'Have they released the name of the victim?'

The barman looked puzzled. Aunt Jessica rephrased her question, 'Did they give any details about the lady who died? Was she a foreign tourist or was she Japanese?'

'Only say her kimono pull open.'

He gave another small bow and went back to his post.

'Sounds like an attempted rape gone wrong, don't you think?' said Curtis.

'How horrible. Can't we talk about something a bit more pleasant?' interrupted his wife. 'Has anyone looked to see what we're doing tomorrow? I know we're catching another bullet train first thing, but I can't remember what's on the programme for the afternoon.'

I felt obliged to buy another round and it was late by the time we got up to our rooms.

'It's been quite a day?' said Aunt Jessica as she scanned her key card across the sensor to open her door.

She left the door ajar which I took as a sign that she wanted me to follow her inside.

'From what the barman was saying, I think there's little doubt that the victim in the park was White Tiger,' I said.

'It certainly looks that way. I think we can assume from her clothes being pulled about that they were searching for the key.'

'The question is, did they know she was the recipient all along or did the real Fox lead them to her?'

Aunt Jessica shook her head in reply. 'That's just one more question to add to the hundred or so already on the list.'

I slumped forward, my head in my hands.

'What on earth's the matter?'

'It's been troubling me ever since you said you thought you'd spotted our stalker. When we first spotted White Tiger, did I give the game away when I tried to race back? Is that why you stopped me? You said something about possible watchers at the time.'

'That was just a precaution. If anyone noticed you at all, they probably assumed you were trying to find another spot to get more pictures. Her death was hardly your fault so stop beating yourself up about it. Besides, I'm not so sure he was following you specifically. As I said before, no one suspicious followed *us* going up that path. If it was the same man as the one in Kyoto, he went in the other direction where most of our lot were heading.'

'I wonder if he was the only one.'

'No way of knowing. Somehow, I doubt it. It rather depends on if Water Dragon knew the identity of White Tiger in the first place and wanted to catch Fox at the handover, and if he knew that's where the handover was due to take place.'

'I suppose so.'

'For all we know, there may have been a prearranged meeting place and time for the hand over.'

'What I can't understand is why the real Fox has never asked me any searching questions about what happened that night when Jewel of Happiness was killed. I know lots of people asked me stuff, but surely the real Fox would have been a lot more persistent?'

'No, I've wondered about that too.'

CHAPTER 17

Aunt Jessica and I were among the first down to breakfast next morning. We helped ourselves from the buffet and I fetched us both cups of coffee from the machine.

'The waiting staff seem excited about something. They're all in a huddle over in the corner,' I said as I put the cups on the table and sat down.

'There's not much for them to do yet. Their job is to clear away the dirty plates, relay the tables and make sure the buffet is kept topped up.'

'I know that,' I said crossly. 'I wasn't criticising them for not doing their job, I'm just saying they seem het up about something in the newspaper one of the girls is holding.'

Aunt Jessica swivelled round in her chair to look at them. 'You're right. Whatever they've been looking at appears to have upset the tall girl.'

'Do you think something's happened?'

'I'll go and find out.'

'Where angels fear to tread…' I muttered softly as Aunt Jessica made her way over.

I watched as they showed her the newspaper and it was several minutes before she returned.

'Is it about the woman who was killed at Itsukushima?' Strange how that word was now beginning to roll off my tongue. Not a place I was going to forget in a hurry.

Aunt Jessica nodded. 'There was a picture of her. Not that I'd recognise the face of the woman we saw, she was too far away, and the victim's name doesn't mean anything. Apparently, she was a very prominent lawyer. She'd made quite a name for herself recently running a very public campaign against various very powerful yakuza bosses. Last month she led a successful prosecution that put one major player in the crime fraternity behind bars for the next twenty-five years.'

My eyebrows must have risen to my hairline. 'Good heavens.'

'From what the girls were saying, the article in the paper implies that her death may be connected to her investigation into a second, but as yet unnamed, criminal mastermind, but there is nothing directly saying that the police have made any statement to that effect. They are still talking as though it was a random attack and she was in the wrong place at the wrong time. The article went on to question if her death will be properly investigated because the man she was gathering evidence about has too many prominent connections in high places in his pocket, including politicians, high-ranking police officers and even media moguls.'

'Do you think that all this secrecy with Jewel of Happiness handing over the key to Fox was related to her investigation?'

'Possibly.' Aunt Jessica frowned. 'It might explain why whoever wanted to pass on information against this man White Tiger was investigating didn't take it straight to the police in the first place. The informer set up this elaborate undercover operation because he felt there was no one else he could trust.'

'It makes sense,' I agreed. 'Especially if he thought he was being watched and couldn't hand it over directly.'

'That's as good an idea as any.'

'What do you think I should do?'

'About the key, do you mean?'

I nodded. 'Even if the police could be trusted, which assuming that article is true, seems highly doubtful, how can I explain why I didn't hand it over when I first found it if I do give it in now?'

Aunt Jessica shrugged and pulled a face.

'So, what do I do with it?'

She picked up her Japanese equivalent of a Danish pastry, took a bite and chewed it slowly, deep in thought.

'Let's hold off for a little while longer until we've got more information, or at least had a chance to think all this through.'

As in the railway station in Kyoto, there were barriers at the edge of the platform.

'The next train coming through is not ours. It's an express so it won't be stopping here,' Gerri said.

'Jolly good,' said Martin. 'That means I can take a video as it goes through the station.'

'Great idea.'

We all lined up behind the barrier, cameras at the ready.

'Here it comes!'

It came. And went.

'Wow!' everyone cried out almost in unison.

'Did anyone manage to get it?' Martin looked around at the sea of shaking heads.

'I managed a photo of the nose of the engine, but it's badly out of focus.' Vincent looked glumly at the tiny image on the back of his camera.

'I knew they were fast, but that was ridiculous. By the time I pressed the button the damn train was gone,' wailed Molly. 'It's amazing because when you're on the train there's no sense of movement indicating just how fast you're going at all, is there?'

I turned to Aunt Jessica to show her my effort, but she had detached herself from everyone else's excitement. Following her line of gaze, I noticed she was staring at Lucy standing by herself way back from the edge of the platform.

'She still looks pretty washed out,' I said quietly. 'Not her usual bouncy self. That fall must have shaken her up more than we thought.'

Apart from my aunt, Lucy was the only one who hadn't tried to get a photo.

'Hmm,' Aunt Jessica murmured doubtfully.

'Or perhaps she just doesn't like trains.'

Aunt Jessica ignored my flippant remark and set off towards the girl. My aunt wouldn't thank me for crowding her style, but I moved close enough to the pair of them to be able to earwig what they were saying while pretending to look at my photos shown on the small screen on the back of the camera.

I missed the opening shot of their conversation, but I caught the tail end.

'…is still a bit sore but my ankle is fine now it's strapped up.'

'So how did it happen? Were you running?'

'No, no, but I wasn't looking where I was going,' Lucy gave a hollow laugh. 'Too busy looking at the phone and tripped over a tree root sticking out of the ground in the middle of the path.'

'It obviously affected you a lot more than you're letting on. You're still very pale and you don't look well at all.'

'I'll admit I don't feel too bright. I didn't get much sleep last night. When I heard about that woman being attacked in the park, I realised how lucky I was. It could so easily have been me. If I'd known there was a madman with a knife charging about the park, I'd never have wandered off all on my own. I know that all sounds a bit hysterical now, but when you're lying there in the dark in the middle of the night all sorts of stupid things go through your head.'

'Why don't you try and get a couple of hours kip on the train? You'll feel better for a good rest and when this place is far behind you.'

The cry went up. 'Here comes our train.'

'We'd better get to the barrier,' Aunt Jessica said. 'If we're not on by the time the doors close, it will be too late. There are no guards and the train won't hang around.'

CHAPTER 18

Our hotel in Kanazawa was another high rise somewhat characterless, inner-city establishment that you might find in any major city anywhere in the world. I confess, after Gerri had told us that Kanazawa had a strong cultural identity and had been shielded from outside influence by its location between the mountains and the sea, I had hoped to find something more distinctive and recognisably Japanese. Nonetheless, on the plus side, it looked a decent, upmarket place and our stay would only be for the one night.

'I'm looking forward to being reunited with my luggage. Do you think our suitcases will already be in our rooms?' asked Gail who was standing in front of me in the queue to check in at the reception desk.

'I expect so,' I said, though why she thought I'd know any better than she did, heaven knows.

I collected my room key and was about to follow Aunt Jessica, when someone called out my name. I turned to see Curtis.

'Where and at what time shall we meet up?'

I had forgotten all about the arrangement he and I had made earlier to talk about his website.

'How about half an hour before the talk? Do you think that will be enough time?'

'I'll bring my laptop with me so I can show you the kind

of thing I'm looking for, and you can tell me if it's feasible. So, where's a good place, the conference room where the talk will be?'

'Sounds good.'

Lunch was at our leisure and on the short walk from the railway station to our hotel, Gerri had pointed out several streets where we'd be able to find something to our taste including some places where we'd find stalls selling street food.

'I'm really not that hungry,' Aunt Jessica said, as we retraced our steps back in the direction of the station. 'How about you?'

'Actually, I fancy trying to find one of the places that does those filled pancakes shaped like a fish that Gerri was talking about.'

'Taiyaki.'

'They sounded rather good.'

'Okay, then let's try down here.'

We'd gone about a hundred yards down the street when we spotted people walking towards us already munching on their purchases. At least, that's what I assumed they were eating as the warm cakes were wrapped in paper napkins. It didn't take long to find the shop. We joined the cluster of people at the open serving window.

'What kind of filling would you like, sweetie? I think I'll go for the red bean paste that Gerri talked about.'

I studied the pictures above the kiosk. 'I can't make up my mind whether to go sweet or savoury. The chocolate or the cheese?'

She gave me a playful punch. 'Live a little. Try the bean paste.'

We took our purchases and I took a cautious nibble as we strolled along the street, then licked my lips. 'Scrummy. I made a good choice there. How's yours?'

'Delicious.'

I took a large bite. Not a good idea. The filling was hot. I fanned my mouth and Aunt Jessica began to laugh.

'That will teach you not to be so greedy.'

'Your sisters would have fifty fits if they could see us now.' I mimicked Aunt Maud's disapproving tone, 'Eating in the street! How very common.'

Aunt Jessica licked her fingers. 'That was very good. Very rich, but I do need a coffee.'

We passed several restaurants but nowhere suitable to buy just coffees.

'There must be a café somewhere. Let's try down one of the side streets,' I suggested.

We turned the next corner and spotted the two Parkes sisters and Josh walking towards us eating enormous ice cream concoctions wrapped in what looked like a pancake.

'Those three appear to have reconciled their differences,' I muttered.

'Those ice creams look good,' said Aunt Jessica when the little group got within talking distance.

'They are. They're from the stall back there, if you fancy one,' said Joanna.

'Actually, we were looking for somewhere to buy a coffee. You haven't seen a café by any chance, have you?'

Lucy shook her head. 'No, but we did pass a drinks machine. You can get a tin of hot coffee there.'

'Tins?'

Lucy laughed. 'Haven't you tried it yet? There are all sorts. Black, white, with sugar, cappuccino, and all sorts of blends. Some have English labels, some with recognisable brand names, but some are all in Japanese and you need to do a bit of guess work.'

'I saw them in Kyoto, but I didn't try one,' I admitted.

'I've developed quite a taste for one Japanese variety. Very different from anything back home.'

We chatted for a few more minutes before going our separate ways.

'Lucy seems to have recovered now,' I said as we walked on.

'Hmm. If anything, it was Josh who seemed uncharacteristically quiet. He's been quiet all morning. He sat by himself on the train whereas on the previous long train journey, he and the girls didn't stop talking the whole time.'

'Perhaps it was because Lucy wanted to sleep.'

'Maybe.' Aunt Jessica didn't sound convinced.

Our afternoon tour took us to Kenrokuen. Our local guide was a smiling young lady with severe black-rimmed glasses and a name I didn't quite catch. I'd been at the back of the group and preoccupied with checking I'd not left my door key card behind when she was introduced.

Our coach dropped us opposite the entrance gateway flanked by pagoda style towers which lay across a wide pedestrian bridge lined with cherry blossom trees. It was a beautiful setting and we were lucky enough to see another couple posing for wedding photographs, she in an orange flower patterned kimono and he in the customary black jacket, grey-striped skirt and white pompom at the waist.

'Spring, in the cherry blossom season, is the most popular time for weddings in Japan,' our guide informed us. 'This is one of the three great gardens of Japan. It dates back to the 16th century and once formed the private outer garden of Kanazawa Castle.'

She led the way across the bridge and through the wooden gateway. The gardens were extensive, with attractive little winding streams and small lakes. We meandered slowly through the gardens where every view proved to be a great photo opportunity. Soon we came to what our guide told us was a traditional tea house where we were to have our tea ceremony demonstration.

We all sat on low benches on three sides of the central area. A girl in a pale grey, pink-flowered kimono appeared and asked for two volunteers. As we'd been warned that the volunteers would be expected to kneel sat back on their heels throughout the ceremony, Isabel suggested this was best left to the younger members and proposed Lucy and

Josh. Josh protested, but with everyone urging him on, he was in no position to refuse for which I was grateful. Though I was possibly a year or two younger than Josh, the idea of being the centre of attention was an even less attractive proposition than sitting for any length of time on my haunches. I was uncomfortable enough sitting on the low bench.

After the customary greetings, our demonstrator talked us through the process as she measured what she called matcha tea powder into her large bowl and added a small amount of near-boiling water. Using a bamboo whisk, she stirred the mixture into a foaming green paste then added more water.

She poured some of the thick pea-green liquid into two tiny bowls which were given to Lucy and Josh. Another kimono-clad assistant brought round a tray with small cups for the rest of us. I looked dubiously at the thick frothy concoction and took a tiny sip.

'It tastes like liquidised raw cabbage leaves,' I whispered to Aunt Jessica.

I noticed I wasn't the only one who replaced an almost full cup on the tray. Japanese green tea was obviously not a favourite.

There was a fair bit of muttering as we all filed out and someone pulled out a packet of mints and started handing them round to those foolish enough to take more than a tentative sip.

Last out were Lucy and Josh, both pulling faces.

'Hats off to our valiant tasters,' laughed Chandler, slapping Josh on the back.

'It was all right for you lot,' Josh said. 'You could all pretend. We had to actually drink the stuff.'

He threaded his arm through Lucy's. 'Where's the nearest of those drinks machines? I desperately need something to take the taste away.'

The two of them raced ahead laughing.

'Josh seems to have livened up now and whatever it was

that caused the rift between those two yesterday morning seems to have been forgotten.' There was no one near but I lowered my voice even more and looked directedly at Aunt Jessica. 'I don't suppose Lucy said anything about it when you were having that little tête-à-tête at the railway station earlier?'

Her lips twitched. 'As it so happens, I did bring up the subject indirectly, but she didn't bite. Just gave an embarrassed laugh and said the two of them weren't joined at the hip.'

'Implying what, exactly?'

'That she seems rather fonder of him than perhaps he is of her? Who knows?'

'Or Josh had a damned good reason for fobbing her off at Itsukushima,' I suggested.

Once we'd left the gardens, the whole group waited by the roadside while our guide phoned for taxis to take us for our final visit of the day, to the town's food market.

I looked around, but no one appeared to be lingering among the passers-by.

'Something wrong?' Aunt Jessica asked.

'Just checking for possible tails,' I said quietly as we both stepped back out of earshot of the others in the group.

She gave me an indulgent smile. 'I think you can probably forget about them from now on. Even if they realise the key wasn't passed on at the shrine, and that one of the party still has it, who can that person give it to now? Whatever secrets that key would unlock, there's no one left to expose Water Dragon, assuming he's the criminal mastermind behind all this. I doubt you are a target any longer. You can relax.'

'What are you saying? That from now on I should forget all about it and just get on with enjoying the rest of the holiday?'

'Is there any reason why you shouldn't?'

'At least two people have died that we know about,' I protested. 'I can't just pretend nothing ever happened.'

'Shush! Keep your voice down. You're attracting attention. All I'm saying is what practically, can you do about it? Where do you go from here?'

'I've no idea, but I can't ignore the deaths of Jewel of Happiness and White Tiger. They deserve better.'

CHAPTER 19

Curtis was already in the room when I went down for our meeting. He'd obviously been there for several minutes because his laptop was fired up and he'd bought up the website creation software on the screen.

'Before you take a look at this in any detail, perhaps I can show you a few of the websites that appeal to me so you can appreciate the sort of thing I'd like to end up with if it's possible.'

'Sounds good to me,' I said. 'Though the thing to remember, creating a website isn't all about pretty pictures and gimmicky popups. You have to think very carefully about what you want it to do for you. If you are intending it to be a marketing tool, what are the essentials?'

The next half hour flew by. I confess, I was quite enthusiastic about the whole concept by the time we packed up. Most of the work I could do on my machine at home, so distance wasn't too great a problem. In any case, Curtis lived in Woking, only thirty or so miles away and on a direct trainline. When I explained that I no longer had a car, he said it wouldn't be a problem as he was happy to come to me.

'So, what do you think? Would you be prepared to do it?'

I turned to him and smiled. 'We'd need to sort out a few more details before I commit myself, but yes, in principle I'd be happy to do it.'

'If it's a question of money, I'm sure we…'

'That's not an issue,' I interrupted. 'To be honest, I'm

quite excited at the prospect. In fact, where money is concerned, you can pay me a nominal figure. If you are happy with the final result, you can give me a good reference and pass my name on to any of your fellow writers you think might be interested.'

I felt quite positive as we all went for dinner after Aunt Jessica's talk. Perhaps life was looking up. There had been no time to give much thought to the project for Curtis, but I already had a few ideas based on the examples of the existing author websites he'd shown me. If I could make a success of this, perhaps he'd be able to persuade a few friends to engage my services. At least it might tide me over for a bit and give me a chance to pay Aunt Jessica for my board and keep.

That evening we shared a table with Martin and Heather, the Australian couple.

'Chandler not with you tonight?' I asked.

'He's not feeling too good. Nothing serious but he decided to skip dinner and have an early night.'

'Sorry to hear that,' said Aunt Jessica. 'I noticed he seemed a bit quieter than usual in the gardens earlier. He's usually busy taking photos whenever I see him.'

Of all the people on the tour, the Stratfords were probably the people my aunt and I had had the least to do with so far. Because Martin's brother was travelling with them, the three usually sat together at meals and few of the Japanese restaurants and cafés we'd used had tables for more than four.

'Have you been to Japan before?' I asked, trying to make conversation. 'It's not so far for you as it is for us.'

Martin chuckled. 'Don't you believe it. It's over five thousand miles from Melbourne. We had a twelve-and-a-half-hour flight.'

'Really! That's longer than us. I'm going to have to study the atlas again. I suppose because there's so little land between the two countries I thought they were much closer.'

'Australia is a long way from anywhere else,' said Heather. 'It makes foreign travel very expensive. It's only since our two kids have grown and left home that we can afford it. Having said that, we've been lucky enough to visit China, Vietnam and Thailand. I've fancied Japan for a long time. It's so very different from anywhere else isn't it? An odd juxtaposition of rigid traditional customs and advanced technology.'

'Does Chandler usually come with you on your travels?' I asked.

'No. This is the first time we've had a holiday together. When we told him we were thinking of coming to Japan, he said it was on his bucket list and asked if we'd mind if he joined us as he didn't fancy doing it on his own.'

I resisted the temptation to look at my aunt.

'Changing the subject,' Aunt Jessica broke in. 'Have you tried using the onsen?'

'Certainly not!' retorted Heather. 'For such prim and proper people, I can't get over how the Japanese seem to enjoy going into a bathing pool stark naked.'

'There is no mixed bathing. It's quite separate pools for men and women. There is a really nice one in our current hotel. You should give it a try. It is part of the culture when all is said and done.'

Heather gave a snort. 'At my age, I am not revealing my sagging body for anyone.'

I bit my lip to stop myself chuckling at the expression on her face. Nonetheless, she glared at me across the table.

'I'm with you,' I said quickly. 'Definitely not my thing either.'

Now that the ice was broken, dinner passed pleasantly. Aunt Jessica and Heather did most of the talking. The pair of them were chatting away about Japanese embroidery when Martin asked me what line of work I was in. Having admitted to Curtis that I was currently between jobs, I could hardly change my story.

'You obviously made enough in banking before you

decided to take a sabbatical. Holidays in Japan don't come cheap. We've been saving a few years for this.'

I was about to say that the travel company was footing the bill for my aunt and me, when it struck me for the first time that it could hardly be the case. In lieu of payment for her services as the accompanying historian, Aunt Jessica probably did get her basic airfare and hotel bills covered, but certainly not mine. With only twelve people on the tour, it didn't make economic sense.

Aunt Maud's condemnation, 'How much longer are you going to sponge on your Aunt Jessica?' came flooding back along with the sudden stark realisation that it was exactly what I had been doing. At the time, though I'd felt guilty for an hour or two, I suppose I'd dismissed Aunt Maud's accusation as just her usual fault-finding. Nothing I'd ever done had come up to the old harridan's expectations. It hadn't occurred to me that her criticism was more than justified. I appreciated that Aunt Jessica's offer for me to act as her general dogsbody on her trip to Morocco was little more than a generous offer because she felt sorry for me, but in the couple of months or so since then, I'd given up my flat and moved in with her. I'd kidded myself that I'd earned my keep by building her a more up-to-date website and giving her lectures a technical slant. I'd also taken over all the household duties. The fact that she'd managed perfectly well without all these things for years was by the way. And she certainly didn't need my help on this trip. For me Japan was pure holiday.

I muttered some non-committal reply and quickly changed the subject.

'You were very quiet on the way back from dinner tonight. Did something happen between you and Martin I didn't catch?'

'No. He seems a nice chap. I was just thinking, that's all.'

'About what?'

I shrugged my shoulders.

'Harry, sit down.'

I sank down on the edge of the bed next to her. She only called me Harry when she was cross or worried about me.

'What is it?' When I still didn't answer, she continued, 'I know this business with Jewel of Happiness and White Tiger is extremely distressing and I appreciate it must be taking its toll on you.'

I grinned. 'I wasn't thinking about them at all.'

'Oh?'

'I know this sounds heartless when they were both murdered so brutally, but I was thinking about me.'

'But without anyone for you to give the key to, there's no reason for anyone to follow you anymore.' She patted my hand. 'I know it's a lot easier said than done but you need to push all of this to the back of your mind and concentrate on enjoying what we've got left of the holiday.'

I nodded then turned to look directly at her. 'Because everything has been such a whirlwind since we arrived, I haven't stopped once to say thank you and tell you how grateful I am not just for this holiday to this amazing place but everything you've done for me these last few months. Not just financially, though as we both know, I'd be on the streets without you, but for all the bolstering up when I hit rock bottom. I can't pretend that I don't need your support for the time being, but I promise when we get back home, things are going to change. I'm going to make something of myself and I'm going to pay you back every penny you've spent on me.'

'Heavens above, sweetie. Where on earth has all this come from?'

I laughed. 'Talking with Curtis earlier, I realised there's lots of people like him, not just writers but other people setting up small businesses who need help not just building websites but with all the technical bibs and bobs, getting their heads round spreadsheets for accounts and orders and using social media for marketing and promotion.'

Her slight frown said it all.

115

'No need to worry. I'm not getting carried away. I do realise that even now, it could all come to nothing, but Curtis is pretty enthusiastic. If it works out well, he said he has a few friends who might be interested in employing my services to help them with the technical side of things. If nothing else, I can make a start on giving you a decent rent.'

'Let's hope it all goes well.' She smiled, but though she didn't say it, I could see she was far from convinced.

CHAPTER 20

Aunt Jessica and I had the table to ourselves at breakfast the next morning. I stifled a yawn as I reached for my coffee cup.

'Didn't you sleep well?'

'I had no problem sleeping, it was just ages before I dropped off.'

She smiled indulgently. 'Thinking about plans for your new career?'

'No,' I said more sharply than I'd intended. 'Actually, I was thinking about Chandler.'

'Oh? What about him?'

'Two things. Doesn't it strike you as odd that Chandler invited himself on holiday with his brother and sister-in-law?'

She shrugged. 'It's a bit unusual perhaps, but perfectly possible.'

'Plus, Martin said last night that Chandler wasn't feeling too good and had planned an early night. But he was full of himself as we came out of the tea ceremony and he seemed fine later when we went round the fish market.'

'Perhaps he drank too much of that matcha tea.'

'I thought it was supposed to improve your digestion, not unsettle your stomach.'

She raised her eyebrows. 'So why do you think he skipped dinner?'

'What if he went to meet someone? Could he be connected to Water Dragon in some way? Did you notice he was the last one back to the group outside the market? We had to wait a good ten minutes for him.'

'I don't think it was that long and he wasn't the only one. Several people got separated inside. The place was like a rabbit warren and it was packed with people. Besides, if as you're suggesting, Chandler met up with someone in there, why would he need to go out again later when the rest of us were at dinner?'

'Perhaps that first meeting was to arrange a time and place for later. Even with all those crowds milling around, there was too great a risk of one of us spotting him and it would be difficult to explain why he was having a long conversation with a Japanese man.' I sat back in my chair. 'You don't look convinced.'

She pulled a face. 'Well it's a possibility, I suppose.'

'But you still think I'm barking up the wrong tree.'

'I think you're wrong about him being a spy in the camp for Water Dragon. As I've said before, the chances are virtually non-existent. There is no evidence that Water Dragon had any idea how the geisha intended to pass the information on to White Tiger until the night Jewel of Happiness was killed. Which means there was no chance of planting a spy among the passengers in advance. But if you are right about Chandler making contact with someone, could it have been an associate of White Tiger?'

'You mean Chandler is Fox?'

'I'm not saying anything as definite as that, only that we need to keep an open mind. Chandler getting lost, then not feeling too good, could be just that. You're probably reading more into it than there is. Let's see what happens today.'

After breakfast we began our walking tour to see the old samurai and merchant houses.

'There's certainly nothing wrong with him now. Quite the life and soul of the party,' I said to Aunt Jessica, nodding at Chandler who was laughing and joking with Martin and Heather near the front of what was now a rather strung-out crocodile.

The guide stopped and waited for us all to catch up.

'We are about to enter the city's higashiyama or geisha district…'

The rest of her explanation washed over me. My mind was still busy trying to work out all the possibilities.

Our guide was the same woman who had been with us the previous day. I still hadn't managed to get a handle on her name. It was a tricky one beginning with an S and four sibilant syllables, but that was as far as I got.

Much of what she was telling us was a repeat of what we learnt in the geisha district in Kyoto and I doubt I was the only one not paying much attention. The geisha district itself was not exactly abounding in photographic possibilities. The wooden panelled walls of the ground floor were virtually featureless, and it was difficult to even distinguish the sliding doors. Only the upper stories had windows forming a continuous narrow strip just below the jutting eaves of the roof.

When we next stopped and gathered round the guide, I took the opportunity to stand so that I could look back the way we had come. Despite Aunt Jessica's comments about there being no need for anyone to follow us any longer, I still had the feeling I was being watched. No one appeared to be holding back waiting until our group had moved on, and as there were no shop windows to stop and gaze at, or doorways in which to hide, any would-be watchers would have to overtake us. There was one Japanese couple with their backs to us. He was taking photos while the woman with him stood waiting, but with so little to photograph even he and his partner eventually turned and walked past us. Neither were distinctively dressed, but as they passed me by, I tried to commit everything about them to memory in order to recognise them again should they pop up again later.

Not that they did. Or at least I didn't spot them as our tour continued to the tiny workshops demonstrating some of the traditional crafts of the area such as kutani pottery and kaga-yuzen silk dyeing. What is it about long floating scarfs that sends women into raptures? The thing that was most fascinating to me was watching the artisans applying fine sheets of gold leaf. Kanazawa provides eighty percent of the country's gold leaf so there are shops with gold covered objects throughout the city. You can even buy ice creams covered in it!

After lunch we left Kanazawa and headed towards the town of Takayama, stopping first on our journey for what was billed in our tour details as 'a washi paper-making experience'. As we all piled off the coach into the workshop, I knew I could forget about any potential watchers for an hour or so.

It turned out to be more interesting than I anticipated. We gathered round great vats of pulp mixture of fibres from the local Kozo tree which is apparently a type of mulberry. We were each given a wooden frame with three postcard sized screens. The instructor showed us how to dip each one into the mixture and shake the water through. This we had to do three times to create the layers.

Then we had to take our frames over to the tables containing boxes of assorted coloured paper shapes and patterns to decorate them. There was a space next to Chandler and I hurried over before anyone else could get there.

'Feeling better today?'

'Sorry?' He gave me a puzzled frown.

'You didn't come with us to dinner last night. Heather said you weren't feeling too good.'

'Oh, yeah. Must have been the smell of that fish at the market. Made me feel a bit queasy. But I'm fine now.' He pulled one the boxes a little closer and peered in at the paper shapes 'What are we supposed to do with these things?'

'The idea is to pick out a couple for each of our postcards and arrange them artistically onto the wet surface.'

He pulled a face and we both laughed.

Once we'd finished, one of the staff came over and took our frames and added a final thin layer of pulp to seal the shapes into the paper. The whole group then went to watch the excess water from our efforts being sucked out by a small machine at the side of the room.

While our postcards were hung up to dry, we wandered round the shop for ten minutes. There were fans, notebooks, small boxes even small bags and pencil cases, but the delicate paper lampshades were what attracted most of us.

I sidled up to Aunt Jessica who was admiring a cylindrical one painted with sprays of tiny pink and pale mauve flowers.

'That would be perfect for your entrance hall, don't you think?' I said.

She smiled. 'That's just what I was thinking.'

'Then let me buy it for you. A token of my appreciation for letting me come with you on this trip.'

Our journey took us up into the snowy pine-covered mountains into an area designated as a national park. At one point the coach crested a rise and we looked down into the valley at the village of Shirakawago spread out below us. The hundred ancient timber houses with their steeply pitched thickly thatched roofs were covered in snow. We all clambered out to take photos.

'These houses are named gassho because the roofs resemble praying hands. Traditionally, they were home to large extended families of twenty to thirty people,' our guide explained.

In the village itself, we visited one of the two hundred and fifty-year-old houses now turned into a museum. The lower floor comprised the living quarters, but upstairs in the loft was a collection of farming implements. It wasn't easy to see up there as the only light came from the small window high up on the side wall at the far end. Walking on the beams was tricky enough in the dark, but it wasn't just my feet I needed to watch. Josh, just ahead of me, swore as he banged his head on one of the roof struts.

I flinched at the impact, it must have hurt, but his violent expletives didn't win him much sympathy. Isabel turned and glared at him and I could hear tuts of disapproval behind me.

There was a chance to explore the village in our free time. The place was designated as a World Heritage site, and Aunt Jessica and I had a pleasant walk alongside the river which was crystal clear with some surprisingly large fish. Ahead of us, we spotted Lucy and Joanna peering into what appeared to be a four-foot-high igloo.

'Do you think the kids made it?' Lucy asked when we got nearer.

'Well if not by them, it was presumably built for them,' Aunt Jessica answered. She bent down and looked inside. 'It's surprising it hasn't started to melt yet.'

'That's true,' agreed Joanna. 'Though how much longer it'll survive is another matter. Despite all the snow up here, it's not what you'd call bitterly cold, is it? Spring is definitely on its way even at this altitude.'

'Josh not with you?' I asked.

Lucy snorted. 'Said he didn't feel too good so he's going to sit in the café until it's time to go back to the coach.'

'That was a nasty crack on the head…'

'The man's a wimp,' she interrupted. 'Any excuse and he pleads he's at death's door.'

Even Joanna looked taken aback by the ferocity of Lucy's anger as she stomped away.

'Sorry, I seem to have struck a nerve there.'

Joanna gave me a rueful smile. 'Don't worry about it. I can see where Lucy's coming from. One-minute Josh is all over her, making a real pest of himself craving her attention, and the next he's making pathetic excuses, changing plans at the last minute. After the tea ceremony yesterday, he pestered her until she agreed to let him treat her to a special dinner just the two of them to make up for being a pain earlier. Then at the last minute, he cried off.'

As Joanna hurried after the fast-disappearing Lucy, I turned to Aunt Jessica.

'What do you make of that?'

'It may be no more than him getting cold feet, but no doubt you have some kind of conspiracy theory. This morning you were all set to label Chandler as the villain and now you want to suggest it must be Josh.'

'I'm just keeping my options open.' There were times when Aunt Jessica's tendency to pour cold water on my ideas became really annoying.

CHAPTER 21

'You're not still sulking, are you?' Aunt Jessica asked as I dumped her computer bag on her bed when we got up to her room.

I thought about pretending not to know what she was talking about, but that would only prove her point. I gave her my best cheeky grin and said, 'Sorry if I was a bit uncommunicative in the coach. To be honest, I was shattered. I'm as certain as I can be that we weren't followed today, but I still can't help looking over my shoulder the whole time. I know with White Tiger out of the picture, there is no reason why anyone should be interested in our party anymore. I keep telling myself to forget all about it and enjoy the rest of the holiday.'

'So why don't you?'

'Two people are dead and for some reason I feel responsible.'

'Why, for goodness' sake?'

'Back in Kyoto, if I hadn't appeared on the scene at just that moment and spooked him would that man have stabbed Jewel of Happiness in the first place? I lie awake at night going over and over what happened. The more I think about it, the more convinced I am that he was there to force her to give him the key, not to kill her.'

'Even if that were true, you can hardly be blamed for the outcome. And how exactly could you have prevented White

Tiger's death?'

I sank down onto the bed. 'I don't know. Perhaps I should have made more of an effort to contact her when we first saw her.'

Aunt Jessica gave a snort. 'Indulging in self-pity isn't going to change anything.'

'I realise that. I know I can't bring either of them back, but I feel I owe them both all I can do to bring their killers to justice.'

'And how exactly do you propose to do that?'

'I have absolutely no idea.' I put my head in my hands.

'You need to work out what you are going to do now.' Aunt Jessica's tone was brusque. 'Unless you can come up with something positive, you might as well forget about the whole thing.'

'Finding the real Fox might be a start,' I snapped defiantly.

'Then you need to work out just how you are going to do that, but right now, I suggest you stop wallowing in self-pity and go to your room and get ready for dinner. We're supposed to be meeting the others in less than an hour and I could do with a long hot shower.'

Perhaps Aunt Jessica had more in common with her older sister than I had ever imagined.

The sky was a leaden grey without a hint of blue when we came down to breakfast next morning.

Molly was in the buffet queue in front of us. 'It's not actually raining, but when Bruce and I went to the front door just now, you could feel the moisture hanging in the air. Gerri said if it rains, the parade will be called off.'

'The procession itself will probably take place, carrying the shrine through the streets with all the monks and the marching bands and so on. It's only the traditional floats that may stay in the storehouses,' Aunt Jessica tried to reassure her.

'But that's what makes it all so special.' Molly's voice rose to a wail. 'A chance to see the giant mechanical puppets was the main reason we chose this tour. Not all the companies actually come to Takayama and it's supposed to be very special.'

'We'll just have to hope for the best.' Aunt Jessica gave Molly a reassuring pat on the arm. 'The Spring Festival takes place over two days so if there is a problem today, we'll have another chance tomorrow. The storehouses will be open in any case, so we'll be able to see the actual floats.'

With a parting smile, she moved further along the buffet table inspecting the breakfast fare. I loaded my plate and followed her to an empty table next to the coffee station.

A fine drizzle meant that the parade of floats was delayed. The main procession carrying the gold portable shrine around the town wasn't due to start until one o'clock, so Gerri took us first to the Festival Floats Exhibition Hall. Once we'd seen a short video telling us all about the festival which dates back to the fifteenth century, we wandered round the display of four of the eleven floats used in the autumn festival. In the next room was a large collection of intricate miniature models of the various shrines.

I was bending down to get a better view of the exquisite craftmanship when a voice suddenly said, 'Have you decided on your prime suspect yet?'

'You made me jump, creeping up on me like that.'

Aunt Jessica ignored my comment. 'Well?'

'For Fox? Not really. Simply because he came on his own, I'd put Josh high on the list, and now we know that this is the first time Chandler's been on holiday with Martin and Heather, he has to be a suspect. But...' I broke off.

'But?'

I gave a long sigh. 'If we're right, and Fox is supposed to be the messenger taking the key from someone in Kyoto to the journalist who can then expose this mafia boss, then I don't fancy either Josh or Chandler for the role.'

'Why not?'

'It's obvious that the key is vital to unlock some kind of evidence. Surely the go-between has to be someone trustworthy. I know you're going to say I'm prejudiced, but of all the people on this tour, I don't trust either Josh or Chandler.'

Aunt Jessica leaned forward to inspect the information panel below the model of the gold-covered shrine I'd been admiring. She was silent for a good minute.

'What do you think?'

There was another long pause before she straightened up. 'I can't say I've spoken with Chandler enough to make a judgement. Josh does appear to be a somewhat shallow and self-centred individual, but that could be an act to throw off any suspicion. At this stage, I think it might be a mistake to rule out any of the others.'

'How do we start asking questions without giving away the fact that I have the key?'

'We are going to have to tread very carefully, sweetie.'

The parade turned out to be everything that the guidebooks and the travel company's effusive blurb had promised and more. The excitement was palpable. One thing that I hadn't quite prepared myself for was the sheer number of spectators. Although the ceremony wasn't due to start until one o'clock, Gerri had made sure we were all at the Hei Shrine a good half hour beforehand. Even then, we had to shuffle around to get a good view of what was happening under the great canopy. Once the drums had finished and the monks set off, it would have been impossible for us all to stay together so we were free to wander around by ourselves. Just keeping next to Aunt Jessica proved to be a difficult task with so many people shoulder to shoulder all fighting to take photos of the procession.

At one point I darted across the road to take a photo of the lion dancers. As they got nearer, I squeezed into a doorway, but a marshal waved me away. I turned to look round for Aunt Jessica. I was lucky to find her. If she hadn't been watching me and waving from the melee of people on the other side of the road, I would've lost her.

It was a great afternoon, but the drizzle that had started just before two o'clock threatened to get heavier which meant that the precious wooden floats had all returned to their sheds. The various groups of bands, dancers and marchers continued, their colourful costumes protected by transparent plastic macs and see-through umbrellas. We were both exhausted by the time we decided to call it a day and head back to the hotel. Though the rain had eased off, it was a surprise to see Lucy pacing up and down by the entrance as we approached. She brushed aside a wet lock of hair sticking to her cheek. The rain running down her anorak had soaked her jeans, the wet material clung to her thighs as it turned the mid-blue material navy.

'I don't suppose you've seen Josh at all, have you?'

'The only people we've come across since we all left the square are Vincent and Gail. I shouldn't worry. Harry and I very nearly got separated at one point when he was busy taking photos. Josh will turn up.'

Lucy responded with a grimace. 'I expect so, but the thing is, he's not answering his mobile.'

'Perhaps he had it turned off. I do that sometimes when I want to save the battery,' I said.

'He wouldn't. When we saw how crowded it was, we agreed we'd phone each other if we got separated.'

'Perhaps he's dropped it. I'm sure there'll be some explanation. You've checked his room, I take it?'

She gave me a withering look.

'Lucy, I really think you should come in. There's nothing you can do out here. You're soaked to the skin. No argument, young lady. You need a hot shower before you catch a chill.' Aunt Jessica locked her arm in Lucy's and marched her through the doors.

I followed in their wake. Lucy's room was on the second floor, and taking my aunt's small backpack, I carried on to the third where my aunt and I were based. Once I'd dumped my stuff, changed out of my wet clothes and hung them up to dry off in the shower, I hovered by the door which I'd left slightly ajar listening for Aunt Jessica's return.

It was probably only five minutes, but it seemed longer before I heard her firm, measured tread coming progressively closer. I looked out as she stopped to insert her key card in the door.

'How is she?' I followed her into her room and put her bag on the side table.

'A lot more worried than I would have expected.'

I took her wet coat and fetched her a towel from the bathroom.

'I can't make that girl out,' I said. 'One minute, Josh seems to get on her nerves, and she wants nothing more to do with him, and the next she acts like he's the love of her life.'

'It does appear a bit like that. Right now, she's worried. Unreasonably so.'

'But there must be a simple explanation for his disappearance. It's a bit over the top to get so hysterical at this stage.'

Aunt Jessica frowned and she said, more to herself than to me, 'Exactly. And Lucy doesn't strike me as the hysterical type.'

Lucy had promised to phone Aunt Jessica the moment Josh returned, but he still hadn't put in an appearance by seven o'clock when we all gathered in the hotel lobby to go out to dinner. No one reported seeing Josh after the procession had begun to move off from the shrine. Gerri made reassuring noises about guests who frequently stayed out watching the festivities which were set to continue until late in the evening.

'If there'd been any kind of accident, someone would have seen him, and we'd know by now.' Whether Isabel's attempt to reassure the obviously upset Lucy only caused more alarm was a moot point.

'The Stratfords aren't here either,' Vincent pointed out.

'All three of them decided to stay in town. Martin phoned me ten minutes ago.' Gerri took a quick count. 'I think that's everyone. Are we all ready?'

As the rest of the party made their way to the front doors, Lucy remained hovering near the reception desk in low, but earnest, conversation with Joanna. Lucy shook her head.

I heard Joanna say, 'There's no point in you staying here. What good will it do?'

Aunt Jessica took charge. 'You girls are coming with us.'

'But I need to…'

'Your sister's right. If there is any news, the hotel reception will give you a ring.' Tucking Lucy's arm through her own, Aunt Jessica marched her towards the door. She caught my eye and I gave her a rueful grin.

'You might as well give in,' I whispered as I fell into step alongside Lucy. 'Cross Aunt Jessica at your peril. Believe me. I'm speaking from experience.'

The four of us found a quiet table and between Aunt Jessica, Joanna and I, we kept the conversation going. I wondered if my aunt would use the opportunity to find out more about what was going on and what Josh might have been up to, but she kept her comments to the floats, the events of the day and the food.

After half an hour, Lucy looked considerably more relaxed and even made her own small contribution to the general chit-chat once or twice. Though he was never mentioned, it was clear that Josh was rarely from her mind. Like me, Lucy had ordered a seafood tempura, but after a few mouthfuls she'd pushed the food around her plate before finally laying down her fork.

Soon after, she started glancing at her watch.

'I enjoyed that,' I said as I pushed my empty plate away. 'How was yours?'

'Very good,' agreed Joanna.

'Then if we've all finished, shall we go?' Aunt Jessica got to her feet.

'Please don't feel you all have to return to the hotel with me,' Lucy protested as we all began to retrace our steps. 'The celebrations are still going on. There's still lots to see.'

'I for one have done as much wandering around the streets as my old legs can take for one day,' replied Aunt Jessica threading her arm through Lucy's and setting off at a pace that belied her last words.

Back at the hotel, all four of us went to reception. Even before we had a chance to ask the question, the young man behind the desk shook his head.

'Mr Rutherford has not returned and there has been no news.'

'Would it be too much trouble to ask you to phone his room? Just in case we missed him earlier,' Aunt Jessica asked giving him a winning smile.

'Of course, madam.'

He let the phone ring for almost a minute before replacing the receiver.

'I know this is very unorthodox, but do you think it would be possible to get a member of staff to actually check the room. Just to reassure us that the poor man isn't in there lying collapsed on the floor.' Aunt Jessica's ability to play the worried old lady who needed to be humoured had the young man rushing to assist.

'Give me a moment and I'll take you myself.'

Having informed his two colleagues, he collected a pass key and led us to the lifts.

Josh's room was on the fifth floor at the end of a long corridor. The four of us waited patiently as the receptionist knocked, called and waited before inserting the key card. He pushed the door ajar a few inches and called again.

When there was still no reply, he opened the door fully and went in. He took a few paces past the door to the bathroom and into the room proper, then stopped.

The women followed. I could tell from the stunned silence and their rigid stance that all was not well.

Fearing the worst, I went in and peered over the heads of the two girls.

The place was an utter mess. Clothes lay everywhere, most still on their hangers flung down in a heap by the wardrobe. Every drawer had been pulled out and the contents strewn over the floor. Even the mattress had been pulled from the bed. Josh's case lay open on the bedframe – not just emptied, the lining had been ripped out. Not a single item of Josh's possessions had been left undisturbed. Nothing had been missed. Even the door of the room safe had been left half open.

CHAPTER 22

An hour later the four of us were still sitting in the bar. Presumably the hotel's other guests were still making merry, enjoying the evening festival celebrations because we had the place to ourselves. Brandy may be good for shock, but it was beginning to make my head ache.

'But I don't understand, why would anyone do such a thing?' said Joanna, not for the first time. I don't think she was anymore used to drinking spirits than I was. It was making her garrulous and her words were becoming noticeably slurred.

I glanced at my watch. 'I wonder how much longer the police will want to keep us waiting.'

'I don't understand why they want to talk to us anyway. We told that officer that we have no idea why Josh's room was ransacked, so what more can we tell them?'

Aunt Jessica gave her a reassuring smile. 'On the positive side, now we've given them a description of what Josh was wearing, we can assume that the police are now keeping an eye out for him.'

Huddled back in an easy chair still nursing her half-full glass, Lucy nodded.

'That's something, I suppose.' Joanna pushed herself to her feet. 'I need the loo.'

Taking a zig-zag path to hold onto the backs of chairs as

she went, she made her way to the door at the far end of the room.

'I don't suppose you have any ideas as to what the intruders were looking for, have you?'

Lucy turned to look at Aunt Jessica's penetrating stare. She shook her head. 'Why should I?'

Aunt Jessica tapped her chin as though deep in thought. Always a danger signal. 'I can't help wondering if this couldn't be connected to everything else that's been going on.'

'I'm not with you.' Lucy sat straighter in the chair.

'You have to admit, disasters appear to be following us around. First a geisha is murdered in the tea house where our party are having dinner, another young woman is murdered at Itsukushima Shrine on the day we happened to be visiting and now someone has broken into Josh's room and torn the place apart.'

'They're random events, surely? There's nothing to suggest they're linked at all.' Lucy's frown deepened.

'If you say so.' Aunt Jessica gave a long sigh and shifted her position. 'I wonder if the intruders found what they were looking for?'

'Money or his laptop. Something they could sell, I expect.'

'I doubt it. You don't eviscerate a suitcase for random valuables. It had to be something quite small, don't you think?'

Any further conversation was cut short as the door to the main hotel opened and two police officers came in.

The trace of a frown crossed the inspector's forehead as he approached.

'Miss Parkes has gone to the bathroom. I'm sure she will be back in a few minutes.'

The slight nod of his head suggested that Aunt Jessica had rightly assessed the cause of his concern.

'Good,' he said, and seated himself on the couch

opposite us. The second officer pulled one of the upright chairs just outside the circle which meant that all three of us would have to turn our heads to look at him. Out of the corner of my eye, I saw him take out a notebook and pen then sit back, presumably ready to take down our answers.

'I appreciate this situation is very upsetting for you all, but there are some questions I need to ask. I will not keep you longer than necessary.' The inspector's English was perfect though the accent suggested he may have spent time in the US. Either that or he'd watched a great deal of American TV.

If his words were intended to be reassuring, he was singularly unsuccessful. I resisted the temptation to wipe my sweating palms on my trousers. Was this the time to tell the police the details of everything that had happened in Kyoto and all the events that had followed? I might be convinced someone was determined to prevent evidence coming to light about corruption in high places, but what evidence did I have? Not even a name! The whole story sounded farfetched. My chances of being believed were zilch.

I tried to let go of the tension I could feel in every muscle in my body and concentrate on what the inspector was saying to Lucy.

'I appreciate that Mr Rutherford was unknown to any of the party before you all arrived in Japan eight days ago, but am I correct in assuming that you and he had become very close?'

'If you are implying that we had some kind of holiday romance, I'm afraid you are mistaken, Inspector.' Lucy was now more in control of herself than she'd been all evening. 'It's probably correct that I spent more time with him than anyone else on the tour, but that was more to do with us being of a similar age. The majority of the group are...' She chose her words carefully possible in deference to Aunt Jessica sitting next to her, 'a little older and tend to retire earlier to bed. Josh, my sister and I often went for a drink after the others had gone up to their rooms.'

'My point is that having spent more time with each other, you might know a little more about him. Can you tell me anything that might help find him or explain why his room should have been targeted?'

'We don't really talk much about ourselves. He's never even mentioned his hometown or where he's living now, but I have the impression he comes from the North of England somewhere. Or at least, was born there.' She turned to Joanna who had just returned.

Joanna nodded. 'He isn't a southerner. Not the way he pronounces his 'a's.'

The inspector frowned and shook his head. 'His home address I can get from your tour representative. I was referring to any personal details such as his family.'

'He doesn't really talk much about himself. He hasn't even mentioned what he does for a living.'

Lucy gave her sister a withering look. 'The whole point of going on holiday is that you leave work behind.' She turned her head back to the inspector. 'Most of the time, people talk about the places they've just seen, and what they liked best and so on. We British prefer not to discuss our personal lives with comparative strangers. In any case, how is any of this going to help find Josh? You already have his height, hair colour and a description of what he is wearing. Isn't that what you should be concentrating on?'

The inspector did not flicker an eyelid at her scathing rejoinder.

'I believe we are at cross-purposes here. Uniformed officers are looking for Mr Rutherford. My concern is why anyone would wish to ransack his room so thoroughly. Though the safe was opened, money and other valuables were not removed which would appear to rule out robbery as a motive. The intruder went to a great deal of trouble to obtain a room key and an override number to open the safe. He or she was apparently looking for something quite specific. I appreciate you may have no idea about what that might be, but I was hoping you might be able to tell me if anything appeared to be troubling Mr Rutherford or if he seemed preoccupied in the last few days.'

We all shook our heads.

'If there is nothing else that any of you can tell me that might help us, I will return to the station. If there is any news as to Mr Rutherford's whereabouts, rest assured the hotel will be informed straight away.'

The inspector rose to his feet and marched smartly to the door, his sergeant scurrying in his wake.

'That's us told,' I muttered half under my breath.

Aunt Jessica glanced at her watch. 'It's gone midnight. Time for bed, I think.'

Lucy frowned and said, 'I need to go to reception. If a message does come through about Josh, I need them to phone me straight away. No matter what the time.'

She was out of the door before the rest of us had time to make any comment.

Joanna shook her head. 'I can't see Lucy attempting to go up to our room any time soon.'

'I agree,' said Aunt Jessica, 'but that doesn't mean you shouldn't get to bed. Don't worry, I'll see to Lucy.'

'But she's my sister.' Joanna's voice trailed off. Aunt Jessica was already halfway across the room.

Joanna and I walked up the stairs together. 'I'm sure everything will be fine,' I said with as much conviction as I could muster.

'I'm not bothered about Josh. He's a grown man, he should be able to look after himself. It's Lucy I'm worried about. I've never seen her like this. The strange thing is, I don't think she even likes the guy. I don't understand what's going on.'

I said nothing. I wasn't sure Joanna was talking to me or just speaking her thoughts out loud.

I left my door slightly ajar as I cleaned my teeth ready for bed in the hope that Aunt Jessica would drop in when she came up. Even if she didn't knock on my door, I would hear her coming and could pop my head out.

Half an hour later, she still hadn't come up. Lucy had obviously decided to wait until there was more news and Aunt Jessica had opted to stay with her. There seemed no point in waiting any longer. Any chat with my aunt would have to wait till morning. I closed my door, turned the lock, got undressed and crawled into bed.

Inevitably, I tossed and turned for a long time that night. Something Lucy had said kept playing on my mind. Although I hadn't questioned it at the time, her comment about people not wanting to talk about their personal lives with fellow travellers was probably overstating things. In my case it was true. I did my best to say as little as possible about my job, or rather the lack of it. Curtis had wheedled my current employment situation out of me but not the real details.

However, on reflection, at this stage in the holiday it was strange not to have picked up a few details about Josh from odd comments that had cropped up in general conversation. Had it been anyone else in the party that the inspector had been enquiring about, I could have offered something. Molly and Bruce Cowell were from South Island, New Zealand and he was a sheep farmer. Vincent Goodman was a history teacher and his wife Gail a ward sister in a hospital in Wakefield and both enjoyed fell-walking and bell-ringing. The Stratfords lived in Melbourne, Martin was a keen fly fisherman and Heather was keen on craft work and was handy with a needle. Isabel helped with the flower arranging in her local church and Curtis had an obsession with steam trains.

On the other hand, I couldn't remember having a real conversation with Josh. He spent most of his time with Lucy and Joanna, but I freely admit, I'd never taken to Josh, so I never went out of my way to exchange more than the odd word or two with him.

Though it was strange, given the considerable amount of

time that the three of them had spent together over the past week, that neither Lucy nor Joanna had gleaned anything about Josh's background. Or were they just not telling?

Josh wasn't the only one who had revealed nothing of himself. Neither had Lucy. All we knew of her was from odd comments that Joanna had made when she had coffee with Aunt Jessica and me one time when Lucy and Josh were off together. Joanna had said that she was a PA in a large office somewhere in London and that Lucy worked for the same company. I had the impression that Lucy was quite senior, but Joanna had not specified exactly what her role was. Joanna was supposed to be the older sister, but she always deferred to her younger sibling and I would go so far as to say she appeared to be in awe of Lucy.

The real puzzle was why Lucy had gone to pieces about Josh? Especially if, as Joanna had suggested, she hadn't really liked the guy.

I'd always been somewhat wary of Lucy. She seemed somewhat calculating to me – not in a devious way, just very sure of herself and clear in what she wanted. A cool customer, so her reaction tonight had seemed totally out of character. And why had she been so snarky to the inspector earlier? She'd been downright rude. If even her own sister had been surprised by her behaviour, it couldn't all be my imagination.

CHAPTER 23

The next morning, I stood outside Aunt Jessica's door uncertain whether to knock. Although we usually went down to breakfast together at seven-thirty, it must have been very late by the time she'd come up to her room. There was a good chance she was still fast asleep.

I glanced up and down the corridor to check no one was about then put my ear to the door. I couldn't hear any sounds from inside, so I tapped lightly. Not loud enough to wake her, but enough to attract her attention if she was up.

There was a trip to some traditional sake warehouses this morning, but the group wouldn't be leaving until nine o'clock, so I decided to let her sleep until I came back up from breakfast.

After all that humming and hawing, both Aunt Jessica and Lucy were already sitting at a table when I walked into the breakfast room. I'd no idea how much sleep either of them had had but neither was wearing the same clothes as last night, so they had obviously been back to their rooms at some point, if only for a shower and change. Lucy looked considerably less fraught than she had last night. She had even regained some colour in her cheeks.

I went to the buffet and filled my plate, trying to decide whether or not to join them. They were sitting at a corner table deep in conversation and hadn't noticed my arrival.

'Hi. Any news?' I hovered behind one of the spare chairs.

Lucy looked up and shook her head. 'Not yet. I asked

one of the girls on reception to ring the police station for me five minutes ago. The inspector is not in yet and there was no one else who could help, but they agreed to leave a message and promised to ring back when they have any information.'

It would serve no purpose to say that sounded like a brush-off. The Japanese are nothing if not polite.

'Don't just stand there hovering, pull up a chair.' Aunt Jessica's smile took away any sting from her words.

I put down my plate. 'Can I fetch either of you a tea or coffee?'

Making conversation was not easy when I finally sat down.

'I hope you managed to get some sleep,' I said to Lucy.

'A little.' She picked up her cup and, elbows on the table, sat sipping. Though, if anything, she seemed more thoughtful than worried.

Aunt Jessica and I did our best to make polite small talk as Lucy played with her sweet bread roll, breaking it into small pieces. There was an empty cereal bowl by her plate, so I presume she had eaten something.

Joanna joined us a short time after.

'You should have woken me,' she admonished her sister as she sat down.

Lucy gave a weak grin. 'You were dead to the world.'

As Joanna continued to quiz her about what time she had come to bed, I returned to the buffet. I had no intention of leaving without a good breakfast inside me. Finding a place for lunch wasn't always easy given my conservative tastes. I wasn't even sure what time we'd be arriving back to Takayama. I hadn't bothered to check the day's itinerary that morning as I usually did first thing. I had a vague idea that we'd be traveling on a local train to the brewery, but, apart from the departure time, I had no idea of timings.

If any of the others in the party had noticed Josh's absence no one commented on it, at least not to us. The room was almost empty by the time the four of us had finished eating.

'Time for me to go and sort myself out,' I said getting to my feet. There was no point asking Aunt Jessica if she'd be coming on the trip. She would stay with Lucy and there was no way Lucy would leave until she had some news. The two of them seemed to have developed a bond.

I was almost at the door when a young woman dressed in a receptionist's uniform stepped into the room and looked around.

'If you're looking for Miss Parkes, she's sitting over in the corner.'

I waited, watching from a distance. The two exchanged a quick word before Lucy jumped to her feet and they both hurried to the door. I stepped to one side and waited for Aunt Jessica and Joanna who were following.

At the reception desk, Lucy took the phone one of the staff handed her. The three of us hovered a few feet away.

'Yes, yes. I'll come straight away.'

Lucy handed back the receiver and turned to us.

'Josh has been found. At least a man answering his description was taken into hospital in the early hours. He'd been attacked and is drifting in and out of consciousness. They need someone to identify him. The inspector is arranging for a car to take me over there.'

'That doesn't sound good.'

'He's been badly beaten up, but he's not on the critical list.'

Inevitably, Aunt Jessica volunteered to go with her. Lucy protested it wasn't necessary, but Aunt Jessica insisted.

'Hospital administration staff can be singularly unhelpful when it comes to giving out information about patients or allowing visitors unless they are close family. With two of us making a fuss, they are more likely to give in.'

Quite what Joanna thought about having her position as her sister's supporter usurped by a virtual stranger, it was difficult to tell. She didn't look unduly put out. If anything, I'd say she was relieved.

'I'll let Gerri know that neither of you will be coming on the trip this morning,' I volunteered. 'Let us know how he is, won't you?'

It was only a short fifteen-minute train ride north of Takayama up into the mountains to Hida-Furukawa. The old city was nothing like I'd expected it to be. When Gerri had mentioned something about a sake brewery, I had visions of wandering around the equivalent of a British brewery or a European winery. The visit turned out to be a gentle stroll through the picturesque streets of this small historic centre. We never ventured inside any of the sake establishments, though the attractive gleaming white earthen walls of the warehouses where the barrels were stored lined a section of the canal district. According to our guide, they dated back to the Edo period and the area hadn't changed a great deal since the nineteenth century.

After the customary spiel from our guide, we had free time to explore by ourselves. The path alongside the canal narrowed at one point and it was difficult to walk more than two abreast. I could see Joanna walking slowly ahead of me. Only occasionally did she glance up at the buildings towering above her or peer into the depths of the canal at the melee of fat golden carp that now teemed in its waters.

I quickened my pace and fell into step beside her.

'You okay?'

'Oh, hi, Harry. Didn't hear you coming.'

'You look lost in thought.'

'Lucy promised to give me a ring, but I haven't heard yet. I don't suppose your aunt has rung you, has she?'

'Give them time.' I glanced around trying to find something to distract her. 'I've never seen so many goldfish all in one place.'

'The guide did say there were four hundred of them.' At least she hadn't been totally preoccupied if she remembered that.

After five minutes of talking about nothing much, we ran

out of small talk and strolled on in silence.

She was the one to break it. 'Your aunt seems to have taken Lucy under her wing.'

I chuckled. 'She does tend to take control.'

'Hmm.' Her face darkened in a frown.

'Problem?'

Joanna gave me a sharp look. 'I'm not jealous if that's what you mean. I'm just surprised that Lucy let her, that's all. Lucy is usually the one to take command of the situation.'

'Perhaps she's fonder of Josh than you appreciated.'

She shook her head vigorously. 'Not after what's she's been saying about him.'

'Perhaps that was just to cover up how she really felt.'

'No, you don't understand. Lucy's a really clever cookie and as hard as nails, she'd never get involved with a narcissistic idiot like him. The only reason she was making up to him was because…' She gave me a quick glance and shook her head.

'Go on.'

'I've said more than I should already. Just forget it.'

We'd reached the Festival Square at the end of the canal. In front of us was the Tukumikan Craft Museum.

'We've still got half an hour before we all meet up again. Do you fancy going in?'

She pulled a face. 'Not really.'

'I can't say I'm that interested in carpentry myself. We heard enough about that in Takayama yesterday. Though there's the Festival Hall across the square there if you want to see more festival floats.'

'I'd prefer a coffee.'

I readily agreed. It would give me a chance to see if I could get any more out of her about what Lucy was up to. 'There's bound to be a café somewhere around.'

Hida-Furukawa didn't attract anything like the number of foreign tourists as its larger neighbour, Takayama, and finding a coffee house was not that easy. Traditional Japanese shops don't have big signs over their doors and from the outside they all look the same. We had to peer through the wooden trellis covering the large windows to work out what might be inside.

We turned off down a side street and saw several people peering through the window of a shop a short distance ahead. Even as we approached, we realised it couldn't be a café from the smells drifting towards us. We joined the spectators.

'Shall we go in? It looks interesting.' It was the first time Joanna had shown any enthusiasm all morning.

We never did get the coffee. We spent the rest of our free time in the candle shop. Watching the process of the candles slowly being created through the various dipping stages was quite mesmerizing. Joanna even bought some.

My chance came on the train back.

'I take it Lucy doesn't have a boyfriend back home?'

'I don't think so.' She saw my raised eyebrow and added quickly, 'We don't live together you know. Truth to tell, I really don't know much about her outside the office.'

'Now I am confused.'

'Strictly speaking we're half-sisters. Same father, different mothers. I was only three when my parents divorced, and I went to live with my mother. Their breakup was acrimonious, so I never saw much of my father, and less and less as time went on. He died of cancer when I was in my teens. Soon after the funeral, Dad's second wife left London and took Lucy back to her hometown of Colchester where she still had family. It was only when I went to work for Carterton International that Lucy and I met up again.'

That explained a great deal.

Joanna took her mobile from her bag and checked once again that there were no messages from Lucy.

'She should have rung by now. She promised to let me know how he is.' She punched the speed dial on her phone. 'Nothing.'

'I expect both she and Aunt Jessica have had to switch

their mobiles off. Hospital regulations.'

Joanna's pinched-lipped expression said it all.

CHAPTER 24

There was still no call from either Lucy or Aunt Jessica by the time we got back to the hotel. Though I said nothing to Joanna, I felt annoyed with my aunt. I could understand that Lucy might not want to leave Josh's side, but knowing how concerned Joanna and I must be, it was surely reasonable for me to expect that Aunt Jessica would think to take a few minutes to pop outside the hospital and give us a quick ring.

The afternoon was free for us all to wander round Takayama at our leisure. I suggested to Joanna that we might meet up again for a spot of lunch, but she brushed me off saying she really wasn't hungry. She said she'd probably see if she could go to the hospital and see what was happening herself. I was about to offer to go with her, but she turned and raced to the stairs before I had a chance to say anything.

I couldn't make up my mind whether that was because she'd had enough of my company, she said more to me than she'd meant to and wanted to avoid me asking any more awkward questions, or she was genuinely worried about Lucy or Josh. Or perhaps all three.

I sat on my bed wondering what to do. There was no way of knowing when Aunt Jessica might return. There was a good chance she wouldn't be back until the evening so there was little point in me sitting in my room twiddling my thumbs all afternoon. I was just about to put on my jacket ready for a wander round the town when there came a knock at my door.

'You're back!'

'Only just. I wanted to catch you in case you were about to leave.' Aunt Jessica sounded breathless. She'd obviously run up the stairs. 'Which I see you are.'

'I'm in no hurry. You said you'd ring.'

'I know. I'm sorry. We had to wait around forever before we could even find out which ward Josh was in. It really doesn't help when you can't speak the language.'

I stood back to let her come in. This wasn't a conversation for the corridor.

'Do you mind if we both pop into mine?'

As soon as we were inside, she took off her jacket, flung it on the bed and dived into the bathroom.

I hung her jacket over the back of the chair, put her bag on the dressing table and sat on her bed.

'Sorry about that. Too many cups of coffee while we were sat about in the waiting room.'

'So how is Josh?'

'In a bad way as far as we could make out. Lucy and I eventually found out which ward he was on, but we couldn't persuade anyone to let us see him. In the end, we found a nurse who spoke enough English to say Josh is still unconscious. Not sure if that's because he hasn't recovered from the beating or because they're keeping him sedated. He has a couple of badly broken ribs and some other injuries. Apparently, they're doing a whole load of tests.'

'That doesn't sound too good. Is Lucy back too?'

She let out a long sigh. 'Sadly not. She was quite insistent that I come back. Said there was no point in me missing any more of my holiday. I did my best, but I couldn't persuade her to come back with me. She was adamant she needed to be there as soon as he woke up. Claimed it was bad enough for him to be waking up to find himself in hospital surrounded by strange faces, but not being able to understand the language everyone is chattering around him wouldn't improve his state of health.'

'She had a point I suppose. So how is Lucy? She seemed

a lot calmer this morning, but she was almost hysterical last night.'

'Back to normal, I'd say.'

'I can't make that woman out at all. If what Joanna says is true, Lucy despises Josh. Called him a narcissistic idiot, so why she's running around after him, heaven knows.'

Aunt Jessica shrugged her shoulders. 'Women fall for the unlikeliest men and vice versa. There's no logic to sexual attraction. Anyway, you were about to go out.'

'I thought I'd try and find a place for some lunch. Are you hungry or do you want to get your head down? I don't suppose you got much sleep last night.'

'I slept very well actually. I was in bed soon after one, dropped off straight away and woke at seven as usual. I thought I'd check up on Lucy but when she wasn't in her room, I went down to see if she was at breakfast.' She took her jacket from the back of the chair, picked up her bag and looked down at me still sitting on the bed. 'Chop, chop. I'm starving. You can tell me all about what you've been doing this morning as we go.'

I hovered by the side of the bed.

'What's the matter?'

Not the best time to ask, but the idea had been rolling around the back of my mind all morning. 'Do you think what happened to Josh and the ransacking of his room were connected?'

'That inspector chappie seems to think so. Muggings are virtually unheard of in Japan. The fact that he still had cash in his wallet but everything that might identify him had been removed suggests it was no ordinary robbery. That and the way his room was thoroughly turned upside down indicates someone was looking for something very specific, don't you think?'

'The key the geisha gave me?'

'Possibly.'

'But why would they think he had it?'

'That's a mystery. You're both roughly the same height

149

and hair colour but he's broad-shouldered and quite muscular and must weigh a good forty pounds more than you.'

'No need to rub it in!' I grinned.

'Let's wait and see if anything more comes to light when Josh wakes up and starts talking.'

Although the skies were still a murky grey, the afternoon was dry which meant that several of the floats were brought out of their warehouses and taken for a short tour around the town. There was no co-ordination between the guilds so there was no procession as such, but the sound of drums and the accompanying musicians could be heard several streets away. Once again, the streets were crowded with eager spectators rushing from one enormous float to another. Trying to find a good spot to take photos and ensure that Aunt Jessica and I didn't get separated was no easy task.

Aunt Jessica had another talk planned for the evening so we couldn't afford to be back too late. While she was looking through her presentation, I went in search of the room the hotel had assigned for us. According to Gerri, who had reminded everyone at the end of our morning trip to Hida-Furukawa, the room was on the ground floor near the breakfast room. The Takanawa Suite didn't live up to its prestigious namesake, Japan's first shogun. It proved to be tiny. True, we were a small group – fourteen if you included Gerri, but we would be hard pushed to position the chairs so that everyone would be able to see the screen. We couldn't project directly onto a wall because large pictures and panelling meant there was no blank space pale enough to use.

I was still trying to arrange the chairs when the first arrivals drifted in.

'This is going to be cosy,' Gerri stood in the doorway. 'Are we all going to fit? Do you want me to go and ask for another room?'

'I think we'll cope. Obviously, Josh won't be coming, and I don't know about Lucy. She might still be at the hospital.'

Gerri shook her head. 'She is back in the hotel, though I'm not sure if she'll be here for the talk.'

'I'll put a chair for her in case.'

'I'm sorry I didn't check on the room earlier. I meant to pop in when we got back at lunchtime, but I wanted to go over to the hospital to see how Josh was doing and I forgot all about it.'

'What's the latest news?'

'He's conscious. He has a broken ankle, a couple of cracked ribs and is badly bruised all over. Lucy said his face looked as though it had been used as a punchbag. She insisted on going in to see him. She made such a fuss, they let her in for a couple of minutes.'

'She can be quite a forceful lady.'

'And how!'

'Did he tell her what happened?'

'To use her words, he either couldn't or wouldn't tell her. She got sent out as soon as the police arrived to interview him. There didn't seem to be any point in staying there after that so we both came back. I reminded her we're all going out together for dinner tonight and she said she'd join us.'

'I take it Josh won't be leaving Takayama with us tomorrow.'

Gerri shook her head. 'He'll be in hospital for a few days yet. I doubt he'll be in a fit state to re-join the tour at all. As soon as he's fit enough to travel, his insurance company will make the arrangements necessary to get him back home.'

The rest of the party were arriving so there was no time for further discussion.

'Do you want to let everyone know how he is before the talk starts?'

Gerri nodded.

'I've just been out to buy a get-well card and a box of sweetmeats. I thought it might be nice if everyone signed it.'

'Great idea. I'm sure he'll appreciate that.'

'There won't be time for me to take it to the hospital, but I'm sure if I give them a generous tip, the hotel will arrange for someone to drop it off for us. The tour company puts enough custom their way when all's said and done.'

Lucy slipped quietly into the back of the room just as Aunt Jessica began the presentation. The only reason I noticed her entrance at all was because my chair was squeezed into the corner. To have any chance of seeing the screen, the chair was sideways on to all the other chairs which meant I noticed the door opening in my peripheral vision.

By the time I'd packed up at the end of the talk, Lucy was long gone.

Although Lucy had regained her control, I felt protective towards her. It wouldn't help if everyone started badgering her with questions.

The restaurant was a typical Japanese affair, not unlike the tea house back in Kyoto with lots of corridors and screen doors separating each group of diners. I must confess, my heart sank when we were shown into our small room. There was a single long low table only a few feet from the ground with two rows of seat cushions one on either side. It was a relief to discover that beneath the table was a deep pit where we could put our legs. It had obviously been designed with their non-oriental customers in mind.

When we sat down, Joanna and Aunt Jessica sat one either side of Lucy, and I made sure to grab the place opposite her on the other side of the table. There were a few moans and groans from the older members of the party as everyone lowered themselves to the floor, but once we were all sat down, no one complained.

Ever the one to strike a positive stance on every situation, Isabel said cheerfully, 'Well this is fun. All part of the Japanese experience.'

There wasn't a set menu so we could all choose what we fancied. It took some time for Gerri to talk us through what was a very Japanese style selection of dishes. Most people went for something light rather than a full meal because like Aunt Jessica and me, they had eaten well at lunch time.

Once all the orders had been taken and the general conversation resumed, Gerri asked what everyone had been doing on their free afternoon. I suspected she was just as keen as I was to avoid any discussion of what had happened to Josh last night. Neither would it help if it became public knowledge that his room had been ransacked. There had been enough speculation already.

After we'd all finished eating and the waiters began to clear away the plates, Gerri announced, 'While I've still got you all here together, just to let you know it's a nine thirty start tomorrow. Don't forget to bring down your cases when you come to breakfast so they can be loaded into the coach and we can all leave for the Kiso Valley on time.'

Heather Stratford piped up, 'Will Josh be joining us?'

'Sadly not. He has broken his ankle, so he'll have to stay in hospital for a few more days yet.'

'What will happen to him? Will he be back in time to fly home with us?'

'I doubt he'll be able to cope too well with the rest of the trip if his foot's in plaster and he's on crutches. Most likely he will fly straight back from the nearest airport as soon as he's allowed to leave hospital.'

Someone arrived with our bills which fortunately curtailed any more discussion about Josh.

I wondered if the inspector appreciated that we were off first thing. There was a good chance I would never find out what Josh's intruder was after or even if Josh was involved in the whole mystery in any way.

CHAPTER 25

I spent another restless night and overslept next morning. I woke to Aunt Jessica's insistent knocking and only had time for a rushed breakfast before our departure for Nagoya. I dozed on the coach for much of the journey to our first stop at the Kiso Valley. Much of Gerri's explanation of the historic significance of this ancient stopping place on the major route between Tokyo and Kyoto passed over my head.

At the head of the valley we all descended from the coach and were given an hour and a half for lunch and to wander down the relatively steep pathway that meandered through the village before meeting up with the coach again at the bottom.

'Have I upset you, sweetie?'

'Why would you think that?' I replied as nonchalantly as I could manage.

'Because, young man, you've hardly said a word to me all morning and you're normally quite a chatterbox.'

'I'm tired that's all. I didn't get much sleep last night.'

She gave a snort. 'You're annoyed because I walked back to the hotel with Lucy after dinner last night.'

'No. Why would that annoy me?'

'Because you felt left out.'

I shook my head. 'Do you really think me that petty?'

'Don't pretend you're not itching to know what Lucy told me. You were so late down to breakfast there wasn't time first thing and, I didn't want to tell you on the coach where we might be overheard.'

'Of course, I do. I'm all ears.'

'Then let's see if we can find a quiet table in here.'

She went over to one of the many café-restaurants dotted along the route and studied the menu.

I looked at my watch. 'It's a bit early yet isn't it. It's only just gone half past eleven.'

'Don't you want to know what I found out?'

She marched up the steps to the entrance. The narrow seating area consisted of two lines of trestle tables and continued up to a second floor perched on the valley side. There were even tables outside looking down onto the main path, but there were no other customers in the top section, so we sat down and studied the menu.

I had to wait until the waitress had brought my soup and Aunt Jessica's imagawayaki, a type of pancake filled with meat, before we were free to talk.

'So was Josh able to tell her what happened?'

'At first he said all he could remember was these two Japanese men coming up to him in the street and the next thing he knew was waking up in hospital. According to Lucy, he seemed very cagey and tried to make out it was a simple mugging, but she obviously didn't believe him any more than you do judging by the expression on your face. By the sound of it, Lucy kept on at him, demanding to know what these men wanted and why they attacked him for no apparent reason. He insisted he had no idea, but when Lucy told him about his room being ransacked, Josh became agitated. He kept saying the sooner he could leave the hospital and go home the better.'

'Did he know what they were after?'

'He said he had no idea. It seems before she could press him any further, the nurse came in and made it obvious Lucy had to leave because Josh was getting in a state.'

'Sounds like he's worried that he might still be in danger.'

'Exactly.'

Aunt Jessica gave me a long look.

'But if they were after the key, why would they think he had it? Surely, as I'm the one who found the dying geisha, wouldn't they come after me first?'

'I've been trying to work that out for days. The only explanation I can come up with is that Jewel of Happiness told her assailant he was too late because she had already passed it on. If you remember, you gave everyone in our party the impression that she was barely alive and incapable of saying anything when you reached her. We know our party was followed for several days. The fact that you were with me all the time and did nothing to arouse their suspicion, like leaving the group to contact anyone, may have convinced them you couldn't be the messenger. Josh was the only unaccompanied member in our group, and he went off on his own on several occasions. We know he went walkabout around the time White Tiger was killed at the Itsukushima Shrine. Perhaps the two of them met up.'

'But if Josh really is Fox, why would he attack White Tiger?'

Aunt Jessica shook her head and glared at me. 'That's not what I meant. If the two were seen together, the assassin may have thought Josh had handed over the key. The fact that the poor woman's clothes were torn and pulled about suggests she was searched. When they didn't find anything, it left Josh as the prime suspect as the man with the key.'

'And as we know, they didn't find it in his room or on his person and, because he couldn't tell them where it was, it means they are going to start looking elsewhere. In which case, I could well be back at the top of their list.'

I suppose I said it in the hope that Aunt Jessica would laugh at the idea and tell me I was being paranoid. She didn't. A cold shiver went down my spine.

'What the hell is this all about? What does this stupid key open and why is it so important that people are dying because of it?'

She shook her head. 'That, sweetie, is the million-dollar

question.'

It was late in the afternoon by the time we arrived at our hotel in Nagoya. After the long day travelling, everyone seemed a little jaded. Our rooms had great views of the town's famous castle. I was still admiring the upturned roof tiers when Aunt Jessica pushed open my door.

'You're not still brooding, are you?'

'No. Just looking at the view.'

She came up beside me. 'It is rather special, isn't it? Built back in the Edo period in the early 1600s, it's one of the largest in the country. However, if we don't go down now, we're going to be late. Are you ready?'

I grabbed my jacket and we headed for the stairs.

Most of the others were already gathered in the lobby. Gerri did a quick head count.

'Listen up, guys. Before we head out for dinner, I just wanted to let you all know I've actually managed to speak to Josh. He says he's feeling much better now. He sounded pretty upbeat. The doctors have now done all their tests and apart from his ankle, there's no major damage, so he's hoping he'll be flying back home in a few days. He wanted me to thank you all for the kind messages you all wrote on the card we sent.'

'That is good news,' said Molly.

There were murmurs of agreement, but I noticed one or two forced smiles.

Chandler muttered something to his brother. Heather glared at him and gave a low response which I only managed to catch because she was facing me and I could read her lips, 'I can't say I took to him either, but there's no cause for you to be so uncharitable.'

Josh obviously hadn't made himself universally popular.

We were joined at our table by Curtis and Isabel.

'It's good news about Josh isn't it? I was wondering how he's going to manage if he's on crutches though. Britain is halfway round the world. We couldn't be much further away. It's an awfully long flight. It was bad enough coming out, cooped up in those dreadful seats.'

'I expect his insurance will pay for him to go business class or even first,' said her ever-practical husband.

'Even so, it'll be hard enough to get on the plane with all his luggage and I should think he'll have to change planes several times. We had a stopover in Dubai coming over, and going home from Tokyo it will be the same. And he's got to get from Takayama to an international airport.'

'The airports will all have staff with wheelchairs for him. It won't be a problem.'

'But when he gets to Heathrow he still has to get back to his home. Doesn't he live up north somewhere? By car that's at least another five-hour journey.'

'You're right,' agreed Curtis. 'However, it's not our problem.'

I wasn't so sure about that.

'Changing the subject.' Curtis turned to me. 'About that website you said you might do for me. I mentioned it on my Facebook Author Page. After what you said before, I wanted advice on the things I need to be up there. The answers I got back have made me realise it's all more complicated than I first thought. They talked about things I'd never even thought of. I'm definitely going to need help. I've also had several comments from my writer friends in the same boat who are also looking for help. Once my website is up and running, I think you might find several more requests and that's just from my group.'

'Really?'

'I know you've been far too busy to even think about it yet, but I've been having a few thoughts on our coach journeys and I've come up with some ideas.'

For the next ten minutes, Curtis and I talked shop. It's true that for the past day or so, with all the excitement over Josh, I hadn't given any thought to my future career such as it was. It was all too clear things couldn't go on the way they were. Jobs were hard to come by, but my chat with Curtis made me think if I could make a success of this, I might have a future doing something that stretched my skills and, more importantly, I could enjoy.

CHAPTER 26

Nagoya, Japan's fourth largest city, is also the home of the Toyota factory.

'I know many of you, the ladies especially, may wonder why the company has chosen to include a car-manufacturing plant on our itinerary. I confess the first time I did this tour, I said as much to my boss. However, having seen it several times now, I can assure you all it really is worth a visit. You will be amazed. Every process is fully automated.'

To judge by a good number of the expressions of the faces of her audience, Gerri's smiling announcement didn't allay everyone's doubts. Including mine, it has to be said. As we filed out of the hotel and into the bus, I overheard several muttered comments which confirmed my suspicions.

We arrived at the factory and had to wait in our coach a good ten minutes for the arrival of our company guide which didn't improve the atmosphere. She eventually arrived, dressed in what looked like a 1950's school uniform with white knee-length socks and sporting a pill-box hat on her head. She welcomed us in a monotone high singsong voice and a fixed smile on her face.

'Do you think she's a robot too,' I whispered to Aunt Jessica and from the giggles coming from behind, the thought had obviously crossed the minds of several of the others.

After an introduction we followed our little manikin to an exhibition hall where there were various sections on environmentally friendly technology, safety and, what was for me, the most interesting one on motor sport. We were then whisked away to one of the giant factory buildings in a company bus to see the main welding and assembly shops. We were led up to the first floor and onto an elevated observation platform looking down on one of the production lines. I had expected each line to be assembling the same model of car but every car on the line was different.

A voice beside me asked, 'How on earth do those robotic arms know which model they're working on?'

I turned to Molly. 'Didn't our guide say something about each car having an identification number that the machines pick up?'

'Wouldn't it be more efficient if they stuck to one model at a time?'

'That wouldn't work with their just-in-time policy. Cars are only produced once the order is made.'

Molly pulled a face. 'I heard her say something about 'just in time' but that voice of hers is so difficult to follow, I can't make out half of what she says.

At the end of the elevated walkway we stepped off into a large space filled with stands of interactive screens. Our Toyota guide thanked us for our visit and reminded us that if we wished to see the robot play its violin, we should be down in the entrance hall just before midday. She presented each of us with a company pen and left.

'Can I just say, before you all start looking around, after the robot has played his piece, we'll all meet back at the coach which will be parked outside near the entrance,' Gerri announced.

Aunt Jessica and I drifted apart while we looked at the various screens. There were also a couple of sports car simulators. By now other tour groups had arrived so there were three or four people ahead of me waiting to have a turn.

'How did you do?' Aunt Jessica asked when I joined her

ready to go back down.

I wrinkled my nose. 'Miserably. Crashed on the first corner on the first run but the second was a bit better. I got halfway round the course before ending up in the wall. I didn't bother with a third try, not with all those people looking on.'

'I thought you claimed to be a good driver,' she teased.

'I am,' I protested. 'Sports cars are very different. The handling is far more sensitive and, whether you like it or not, you're going at a speed way faster than I'm used to.'

There was already quite a crowd assembled around the alcove where the four-foot high robot was standing. I managed to squeeze into a space on the third row where I could just about see over the shoulder of a bulky six-foot man. At five nine, I don't consider myself short, but the first couple of rows seemed to be dominated by giants.

On the stroke of twelve o'clock, the robot took a few steps forward and flourished his bow above his head. He then proceeded to play of all things, "Land of Hope and Glory". It probably wouldn't have won him a place in any symphony orchestra, but it was nonetheless a very creditable performance. An amazing piece of engineering which demonstrated, as if what we had witnessed on the production line was not enough, just how precise robot technology can be.

At the end of the performance, people began to drift away, and I had a moment of panic when I couldn't see Aunt Jessica. I told myself not to worry. Like everyone in our group, she'd be heading for the exit doors and I'd meet up with her at the coach. Looking around, my heart stopped momentarily when I thought I recognised the face of a man on the far side of the room staring straight at me. Our eyes met for a brief moment before he turned and disappeared into the crowd before I had a chance to react.

I spotted Aunt Jessica with Lucy both trying to make their way past some noisy teenagers pushing through to the start of the tour. My shirt was clinging to my back by the time I'd managed to edge my way through the mass of bodies funnelling through the exit door and get outside. The crowds fanned out across the parking area to the lines of waiting coaches. Our minibus was off to the right and I spotted Lucy's blonde pigtail swinging from side to side as she kept turning to speak with Aunt Jessica some distance ahead. Taking advantage of a break in the traffic, I stepped into the road and overtook a few people until I was only a few yards behind them, separated only by Vince and Gail Goodman who were strolling along hand in hand taking up most of the path. Much as I was eager to tell Aunt Jessica about my sighting of our stalker, I decided to hang back and wait until we got on the coach. I could hardly ask if she had noticed him too with Lucy standing beside us. My heart was beginning to return to normal and I was already having doubts. My glimpse had been far too brief to be certain the man was our watcher.

Aunt Jessica was looking pretty pleased with herself as I slid into the seat alongside her.

'Something to tell you when we stop,' she whispered with a definite gleam in her eye.

Before I could reply, there was a call for hush as Gerri informed us what we'd be doing for the rest of the day.

The next thing on our itinerary was lunch so I had to curb my impatience to share my tale for another half-hour. She was right as usual. The minibus was far too public to discuss sensitive matters in any case. At least trying to think what could have made her so excited kept me from frightening myself further with thoughts that once again we were being followed.

Any hope of a private chat in the restaurant were quickly dashed. The seating was all at tables for six and Gerri quickly commandeered two tables so we could all sit together.

Lucy and Joanna sat at the second table with the other Brits and we shared a table with the guys from Down Under, Bruce and Molly Cowell and the three Stratfords, Martin,

Heather and Chandler.

I squeezed in an extra chair and sat down.

'What did you all think of it?' asked Aunt Jessica. 'Was it what you expected?'

'I'm still not convinced that the girl showing us round wasn't actually a robot,' said Martin. 'When I asked her a question, she just continued with the company spiel she'd learnt by rote which had very little to do with what I'd asked her.'

'Her voice did sound very mechanical,' agreed his wife nodding her head. 'And did you notice all the guides looked exactly the same? Not just their uniforms but their hairstyles, they were more or less the same height and had the same expressions on their faces.

'Lack of expression, more like,' said Chandler.

For the next ten minutes we all talked Toyota, but the general consensus was that the visit was enjoyable.

'It does show you another side of Japan, doesn't it?'

After lunch, the minibus took us to the station. Much of the afternoon would be spent on the train travelling to Hakone.

The comfortable bucket seats on the bullet train had the added advantage of high backs which afforded Aunt Jessica and me a degree of privacy. As long as we kept our voices low, there was little chance of being overheard.

'Are you okay, sweetie? You hardly spoke over lunch and you still look very pale.'

'I was worried coming out of the factory. One minute you were right beside me and then you'd disappeared. I thought I'd lost you.'

'Sorry about that.' She gave me a big grin that belied her words. 'I saw a chance to get Lucy on her own and I wanted to ask if she'd heard from Josh.'

'And had she?'

She nodded. 'He said he didn't remember much about the incident itself, but he seemed pretty irate with the inspector. He told Lucy that the man badgered him over and over about what his attackers wanted. Josh told him he had no idea, but the inspector kept on at him. Said the fact that his hotel room had been turned upside down had to mean he'd crossed someone while he was over here.'

'You can see the inspector's point.'

'Lucy said Josh was getting more and more angry as he told her the story. Then he said that after the inspector had gone, he did remember something. The two men demanded he hand over the notebook.'

I was so surprised, I blurted out, 'Notebook!'

After she'd shushed me, she continued, 'Lucy asked what notebook and Josh said he had no idea, which is what he told the men. He claimed the men were insistent that even if he didn't have it then he must know where it was. At that point, one of them punched him in the stomach, and he thinks they used the word USB stick. When he protested that he had no idea what they were talking about, the other one gave him a violent blow on the head sending him to the ground.'

'Did he tell the police all this?'

'That's just what Lucy asked, but Josh said no way, not after the inspector had given him such a hard time. She seems to think his attackers may have threatened him to keep his mouth shut. She told him that if he didn't feel safe, he should ring the inspector straight away as it might help the police catch whoever had done it, but he just muttered something about the sooner he could get on a plane home the better.'

'That might be a while yet.'

Aunt Jessica shrugged her shoulders.

We were both quiet for a while until she suddenly asked, 'You're still looking peaky. Sure you're alright?'

'I'm fine.' After a pause I said, 'I don't suppose you noticed if anyone was showing any interest in us when we were watching that robot violinist, did you?'

'No. I presume you saw something.'

I told her of my suspicions.

'I doubt it was the same man. If whoever is behind all this has this much invested, I very much doubt he'd use the same people he used in Kyoto if only because we might recognise them.'

'That's not reassuring.'

She patted my hand. 'If it's any consolation, I have been keeping a close eye ever since Josh was attacked.'

'Why didn't you say?'

She gave a long sigh. 'I thought you were worried enough already and if you started looking over your shoulder for possible shadows, you were more likely to draw attention to yourself.'

I was about to protest but I had to concede, she had a point. I stared out of the window, but my mind was still in turmoil.

'What I don't understand is why they attacked Josh. I was the one who found Jewel of Happiness not him.'

'Shh,' she said sharply. My voice must have risen. 'Let's talk when we get to the hotel. For all we know, Josh going home might be the end of it. For now, just sit back and enjoy the ride.'

Easier said than done.

CHAPTER 27

I'd slept on the last part of the journey and was feeling much better by the time we reached the hotel. Gerri gave us a short briefing about our dinner arrangements and once we had our keys we went in search of our rooms. Aunt Jessica opened her door.

'My goodness me. Gerri said we'd be in a Japanese style-room but look at this.'

I followed her into a small entrance lobby. On one side was a shoe rack containing half a dozen pairs of slippers and beyond the half open sliding doors facing us, we could see a large room with a low table in the centre with four legless chairs with padded seats and backs.

'How many people are staying in here?' I joked. 'What's in here?'

On the other side of the lobby was another set of sliding doors. I pulled them open to reveal a set of floor-to-ceiling shelves.

We dropped the luggage, pulled off our shoes and changed into slippers, eager to explore.

There was a short corridor leading to several small rooms.

I slid open the door to the first room which contained a toilet and small sink. 'There's more slippers here,' I called out. 'This is the first hotel I've ever stayed in where you have to change your shoes to use the loo!'

Aunt Jessica was in the bathroom inspecting the spa bath

and large shower cubicle.

'Where's the sink?'

'At the end of the corridor.'

'So where is the bedroom?'

She laughed. 'Let's go and find out.'

We retraced our steps and went into the main room.

'This is all very traditional. See the shrine over there.' She pointed to a small alcove. 'And just look at that view.'

The sliding panels covering the windows had been drawn back and, in the distance, we could see the snow-capped peak of Mount Fuji.

'Breath-taking!'

Sliding a few more panels we discovered the bedroom. A large double futon mattress lay on the floor taking up most of the space.

'I wonder if my room is the same. I'm just going to take my stuff next door and see. Back in a tick.'

Our main cases had been taken straight to Tokyo, so it didn't take long to unpack my overnight things. When I got back, Aunt Jessica was sitting cross-legged on one of the chairs at the table with her laptop open in front of her.

'Come and join me.'

There was no way I could sit with my legs crossed but the table was just high enough to stretch them out underneath. I leant back and gave a contented sigh.

'This chair is a lot more comfortable than I imagined it would be even if it hasn't got legs. Are you all ready for tonight? If you want to prepare your lecture, I can always go back to my room. I promised Curtis I'd come up with some design ideas for his website.'

'How's that coming along?'

'I've made a few sketches, but I can't do much until I get home and have done more research.'

'Do you think you'll go ahead with it?'

'Definitely. To be honest, I'm quite excited about it. It's right up my street and you never know; it could turn out to lead to further possibilities.'

She didn't look totally convinced.

'What people like Curtis need is not one of these big remote agencies that provide complete packages but a personal service. Someone who can actually sit alongside them at their own computers helping them work through stage by stage so they can understand what they are doing.'

'I take your point, sweetie. You can have a reference from me for a start. You've done a good job with my website.'

I wrinkled my nose. 'I know I'm getting carried away, but I really think I can make it work. If I can get a few commissions to start with, I might be able to put enough by to do a design graphics course and get some qualifications and set myself up as a freelance consultant. It's what I always wanted to do. Do you remember the furore there was when I said I wanted to do that media design degree at UEA?'

'I remember your mother in tears on the phone to me asking for my advice. She didn't know what to do for the best. Maud and Edwina were both adamant that it was a Mickey Mouse degree and it wouldn't help you get a decent job once you'd qualified.'

'And what did you say?'

'That you were eighteen and old enough to know your own mind and that she should let you make your own decisions.'

'With both her other sisters on at her, Mum caved in. With both Aunt Maud and Aunt Edwina telling me on a daily basis how much I was letting down my mother by going against what she knew was best for me on a daily basis, and with no one to stand in my corner, I eventually gave in too.'

'I would have supported you!'

'You were in Uzbekistan at the time, I seem to remember. Anyway, no use mooning about what might have been, I'd better get to my own room and give you a chance to run through your notes for your talk. It's the last one tonight, isn't it?' She nodded. 'I'll give you a knock fifteen minutes beforehand to collect the laptop and all the leads to set up in plenty of time.'

The phone rang just as I was about to leave.

Aunt Jessica picked up the receiver as I walked to the door. I turned to give her a goodbye wave when she beckoned me back.

'Actually, he's right here with me. I'll pass you over.' Putting her hand over the mouthpiece, she turned to me and said, 'It's reception. They want to speak to you.'

I raised my eyebrows and took the receiver.

'This is Harry Hamilton-James.'

'Good evening, sir. This is reception, I have a Chief Inspector Sakamoto asking for you. Is it possible for you to come and speak to him, please?'

'Erm, yes, of course. I'll be straight down.'

I relayed the conversation to Aunt Jessica. 'I wonder what they want?'

She sensed my tension. 'I doubt they are going to arrest you, but I'll come with you if you like, for moral support.'

It was tempting, but I did my best to give a nonchalant shrug. 'It's fine. I don't need my hand holding. Besides, haven't you got your talk to go through?'

'True, but you know what a nosey parker I am. I couldn't concentrate on the decline and fall of the shogunate in the nineteenth century when I'm dying to know what's happening. I'll follow you down and I promise I'll stay on the side-lines and not interfere.' I knew she'd only offered for my sake, but there was no way I was going to tell her not to bother.

CHAPTER 28

Two men dressed in smart business suits were standing by the desk as I approached. The older man stepped forward his hand outstretched. 'Mr Hamilton-James?'

I nodded and took his hand.

'First let me introduce myself. My name is Chief Inspector Sakamoto, and this is my colleague, Sergeant Takahashi. Shall we sit down?' He led the way to a secluded group of easy chairs.

As soon as we were all seated, he continued, 'You must be wondering what all this is about. We are investigating an incident that took place in Kyoto on the ninth of this month. I understand you were present at the fatal attack on Yoshida Noa, the geisha whose professional name was Jewel of Happiness.'

'I was,' I replied guardedly.

He smiled. 'I would like to ask you a few questions about what you witnessed.'

'I have already given a very full statement to the Kyoto police.'

'I appreciate that, but it frequently happens that witnesses who have experienced such traumatic events may recall things after a few days that did not spring to mind at the time.'

'After my interview, Inspector Hamamoto gave me his card and asked me to get in touch with him should I remember any other details.'

'It would help us considerably if you would tell us what happened from the moment you became involved. It might help bring back something you may have forgotten.'

His broad smile failed to reassure me. It wasn't only that the smile didn't reach his eyes, it was the fact that he was trying just a bit too hard.

I glanced up and saw Aunt Jessica sitting in a chair a few feet away, ostensibly reading a book. What would she do in this situation?

I looked back at the chief inspector and gave a meaningless polite smile of my own. 'You will forgive me, gentlemen, but may I ask you to show me your identification?'

Without hesitation, he pulled out a card. Not that it was any help. It was all in Japanese characters. It could have been his driving licence for all I knew. His colleague showed me a similar card.

He must have seen my scepticism. 'As you see, we are not with the Kyoto force. We are members of the Special Investigation Department based in Tokyo looking into a very different matter – a case of corruption.'

'Tokyo? Hakone is a somewhat outside your jurisdiction, isn't it?'

The slight purse of lips indicated his annoyance at my questioning of his authority. 'The Special Investigation Department has a nationwide brief. We believe our case may be connected to the incident you witnessed.'

'In what way?'

'That I am not at liberty to tell you, though I will say that there is a strong possibility that it may be linked to other incidents that have occurred which you might also be aware of. Anything, no matter how inconsequential it might seem, may help us to bring one of this country's major criminals to justice.'

I sat back in the chair and crossed my legs, easing the tension that had built up in my shoulders. If they really were investigating corruption, I could pass on the key and let them get on with it. I looked across at Aunt Jessica. I'd prefer to talk things over with her before making any rash decisions.

'What specifically do you want to know?'

'Let us start with how you came to be in that part of the tea house. It is not in the public area.'

I gave him the bare details.

'The man who attacked her, would you recognise him again?'

'No. He glanced at me for only a split second before he turned to get away.'

'And the geisha, was she still alive when you reached her?'

'Barely. She was still breathing, but she died less than a minute later before help arrived.'

'Did she say anything before she collapsed?'

Now I was in more difficult territory. 'I think she was trying to, but it was difficult to work out what it was, and in any case, I was busy trying to stem the blood spurting from her chest.'

'Are you certain she gave you no names?'

'I don't speak Japanese. I wouldn't know.'

'Think hard, Mr Hamilton-James. Can you recall anything at all? It could be vital.'

I still wasn't convinced that this so-called Detective Chief Inspector Sakamoto really was who he said he was. 'I'm sorry, I really can't help you.'

The false smile never left his face. He didn't ask if she'd given me anything and I decided not to volunteer anything else for now.

'Who was the first to arrive after you had shouted for help?'

'My aunt. She had come looking for me.'

'And after that?'

'I'm not sure. Some staff arrived and then the maiko was there.'

We all sat in silence for a moment or two before he

asked, 'One final question, Mr Hamilton-James. Did you pass anyone in the corridor coming back from the rear of the teahouse?'

I shook my head. 'No. Otherwise I wouldn't have got lost in the first place, would I?'

He nodded in acknowledgement. He took a card and a pen from an inside pocket of his jacket and wrote something on the back. 'This is my personal number on which I can be reached at any time. If you do recall anything else of importance, please get in touch.'

He stood up and handed me the card. 'Thank you so much for your time, Mr Hamilton-James.' He took a step back, clicking his heels, and gave me a low bow.

He and his silent colleague were already walking to the exit door before, lacking the natural agility of the Japanese, I had time to push myself up from the low bucket chair.

'Why didn't you just hand over the key?'

I shrugged my shoulders. 'Gut feeling, I suppose. Can't explain why exactly, but I just didn't trust him.'

Aunt Jessica pulled a face. 'This was a chance to pass the whole affair over to someone else and let them take care of it.'

'I know. I'm still not sure if I've done the right thing. I just need more time to think it over.'

'What was it about him that you didn't trust?'

'For a start his whole manner was wrong for a policeman. All of the ones I've had dealings with have kept things official. He was smarmy – trying too hard to put me at my ease. Too persuasive.'

'Why wouldn't he be? You weren't a suspect. Let's face it, your experience of the police has been pretty limited. You've been watching too many of those TV dramas with aggressive cops trying to bludgeon a confession out of known criminals. Not all policemen are like that.'

'His eyes never left my face, observing my every reaction.'

'Just what you'd expect from any policeman.'

'Well yes, but when I said Inspector Hamamoto had given me his card, I deliberately didn't say if I'd rung him back. It was pretty clear Chief Inspector Sakamoto had no idea if I had or not and he changed the subject. If he was who he said he was, he would've made it his business to find out.'

She didn't look convinced.

'Plus, from the little I'd observed during my time here, like all Japanese officials, their policemen tend not to show any emotion, nor do they shake hands but give a polite bow.'

'Are you sure you're not overreacting?'

'You were too far away to judge.'

'Granted.'

'I want a bit of time to think it all over. I've got his number so I can always ring him back. Or better still, I could get the number for the Special Investigation Department in Tokyo and ring to ask for him by name and see what happens.'

'Good luck with that.'

Much as I resented her pouring cold water on what would be a great way to check on the man's credentials, I had to concede the chances of me getting hold of the number and then communicating my request when I didn't speak the language were not great.

'Anyway,' I said, 'it's time we thought about getting downstairs before we're late for your lecture.'

There was only a short interval between Aunt Jessica's talk and dinner. Tonight, there was to be a special Japanese kaiseki meal in the hotel in a private room so there was no opportunity for us to discuss Detective Inspector Sakamoto any further. In keeping with the traditional atmosphere, we all had to change into blue kimonos and wear special yukata slippers.

Rather like the meal we had had in the tea house, it consisted of a collection of small dishes, each artistically arranged and laid out at each place setting on either side of a long table. Again, there were no serving staff, but Gerri talked us through the order in which each dish should be eaten.

Attractive though it all looked, I confess there was little to tempt my appetite. Despite Aunt Jessica's teasing about my conservative tastes in food, I was prepared to try new dishes, but my stomach balked at the sight of the large snail on the plate in front of me. It appeared I was not the only one, Molly who was sitting opposite me, discreetly popped hers on her husband's plate.

'Do you like snails?' I asked Bruce.

'Love 'em.'

'In which case…'

That started a flood. 'Whoa! I like the things, but enough's enough.'

It may not have been my favourite meal of the holiday in terms of the food, but in terms of social camaraderie, it was the best yet. Everyone was in high spirits. Even Chandler, who usually kept himself very much to himself, joined in the jollity. The sake flowed freely, and it turned into an evening packed with laughter and bonhomie. So much so that it was almost midnight before we all made our way to bed.

CHAPTER 29

It was an early start next morning and there were several empty seats at breakfast. Vincent even came down wearing his sunglasses and a hangdog expression.

'Someone drank too much sake last night,' I whispered to Aunt Jessica as I piled my plate at the buffet.

'Stop gloating, you obnoxious child! Just because you don't like the stuff and remained disgustingly sober.'

'Seems he's not the only one.' I couldn't resist a smile as I nodded at the single roll on her plate. 'Is that all you're having?'

'I'm not feeling that hungry this morning, but I do *not* have a hangover if that's what you're implying.'

'Of course not.' My grin spread from ear to ear as we sat down. 'Perhaps that oyster didn't agree with you.'

'There was nothing wrong with the oysters though I'll agree, it was probably a mistake to have eaten so many.' The snails were not the only things that got passed down the table last night. 'But it did give me the opportunity to have a word with our mysterious loner.'

'Chandler?' I'd noticed that he'd been sitting on Aunt Jessica's left though I'd heard nothing of their conversation.

'Uh-huh. We struck up a conversation when he gave me his oyster. All that booze had loosened his tongue somewhat. He let slip a piece of interesting information.' She paused and took a long draught of her coffee.

'Don't keep me in suspense.'

'I said something about it being a pity Josh was no longer with us.'

I frowned. 'But those two never did get on.'

'That's why I said it – to see what his response might be. It worked even better than I'd hoped. He muttered something about Josh not being the blue-eyed boy everyone thought he was. I asked him what he meant, and he made a remark about Josh sneaking off half the time and up to no good.'

'That's rich, coming from him. Chandler's forever going off on his own.'

'Ahh, but here's the interesting bit. According to Chandler, he saw Josh acting very suspiciously late in the afternoon on the day he went missing. Seems Josh was heading away from all the parades and celebrations and into the back streets. Chandler admitted he followed to see what Josh was up to and he saw him meet up with two Japanese men. They talked for a minute or so and all three of them disappeared inside one of the wooden houses.'

'Why didn't he tell the police that when everyone was looking for Josh?'

'If you remember, it was only after we discovered Josh's room had been ransacked later that evening that the police became involved. Everyone else was out enjoying the celebrations. They had no idea he was missing at that stage. By the next morning Josh had been found so I don't suppose the police asked any of the rest of the party.'

'I suppose not. What do you think Josh was up to?'

'We only have Chandler's word for it that Josh had planned to meet up with these two men. It could have been a chance encounter. Perhaps he was lost and stopped someone to ask directions.'

'But why would he have gone into a building with them? Could they have been the two who beat him up, do you think?'

'Do you mind if we join you?' Neither of us had noticed Isabel and Curtis approaching our table.

'Of course not.' Aunt Jessica looked up at them with one of her beaming smiles.

I could only hope my frustration didn't show in my expression.

There was no time to talk after breakfast. We had to pack all our stuff because after the morning tour to a volcanic area south of Mount Fuji we were off to the station for the bullet train to Tokyo.

The steep walk up to the volcanic crater did give some wonderful views and interesting though the hot springs were, it was difficult to give everything my full attention. There were too many questions running around my head.

At one point we stopped to watch them cooking eggs in one of the boiling pools. The eggs came out with their shells blackened by the sulphur. We were told that eating one of the eggs would prolong our lives by seven years. Down in the shopping area by the entrance to the park, the kiosks selling the eggs were doing a roaring trade. I bought one for its curiosity value – not to eat but to take home to my mother. I also decided it was high time to send her a postcard and a picture of Mount Fuji seemed particularly appropriate. The main shop also sold stamps. It even had a post-box.

Once we had boarded the bullet train and settled in our seats, Gerri came to check all was well. There had been little on offer in the way of lunch up at the volcanic park so, like the rest of our party, Aunt Jessica and I had opted to buy bento boxes from the shops in the railway station.

'I must admit, I'm really quite hungry.'

Tempting though it was to tease her for not having a decent breakfast, I simply gave her a broad smile and inspected the contents of my box. I'd managed to find one, clearly designed for western visitors, where I could recognise ninety percent of the items. I munched the salad occupying the bottom corner and began on the chicken breast pieces covered in a thick brownish sauce that the girl behind the counter had assured me was sticky plum.

'This is good,' I said twiddling the noodles around my plastic fork.

Only when we'd finished eating and sat back could I bring up the subject again. We were sitting in the back seats of the carriage so there was no chance of anyone behind us listening in to our conversation. In front of us, Curtis and Isabel were playing cards. Across the aisle in the window seat, Molly was watching the countryside go by and Bruce was doing a crossword. Both were listening to their MP3 players and were wearing earbuds. Nonetheless, I kept my voice low.

'What do you think Josh was really up to that last evening?' I asked.

Aunt Jessica turned her head to look straight at me. 'Look, Harry, before we go any further, I need you to think about the consequences of what you're doing. This isn't a game. Two people have already died. This Water Dragon has a powerful network behind him. I promised your mother I wouldn't let you get into any trouble...'

'Is that why you keep trying to put me off, telling me to hand over the key?'

'If you're serious about trying to get to the bottom of all this, I'll be right behind you, but make no mistake, we're moving into dangerous territory.'

'So, what do we do now?'

'It's time to stop speculating and reacting to each event as it happens. We've been so busy trying to identify Fox that we've forgotten the bigger picture.' She rooted in her tote bag and pulled out a large sheet of blank paper and her pencil case. Pushing aside the discarded lunch boxes, she said, 'Let's take a step back and make a list of the things we know for certain, then what we are reasonably sure of and see if we can fit the pieces together.'

At the centre of the page, she wrote Jewel of Happiness.

'Before she died, Jewel of Happiness gave you three

names – Fox, White Tiger and Water Dragon.' Adding the names and lines, Aunt Jessica began to build up a spider diagram.

'Though we don't know the identity of Fox, it's safe to say, he is the messenger. Believing you were Fox, she gave you a key with instructions to take it to White Tiger.'

She pulled out a handful of different coloured pencils and choosing a red one, drew a line connecting the two names and printed the word key along it.

'Jewel of Happiness told me to beware of Water Dragon, so can we assume that he was the one behind the events that led to her death?'

She nodded. 'It also explains why White Tiger's clothes were all over the place. Her body was searched for the key. Which leads us to the next logical question, why is Water Dragon so keen to get hold of the key that he's prepared to kill for it? We know that White Tiger was a leading journalist who'd made it her mission to expose corruption in high places.'

'Which suggests that Water Dragon is at the heart of that corruption. Probably the mastermind behind the whole business.'

'Exactly. Whatever that key opens must contain evidence that blows his whole operation apart.'

'How does what happened to Josh fit in? Was he or wasn't he the real Fox?

'I'm not sure that matters any more. What is important is that Water Dragon thought he was. But we know he still doesn't have the key.'

I gave a long sigh. 'So, where do we go from here?'

She tapped the pencil against her teeth. After what seemed an eternity, she said, 'I think there are several questions we need to ask ourselves including how did Jewel of Happiness get hold of the key in the first place, but the most pressing of all, what does Water Dragon do now, because as sure as the Pope's a Catholic, he's not going to give up.'

'How in heaven's name can we work that out?'

She sat back and looked at me. 'What would you do if you were Water Dragon?'

I took a moment to think it over. 'Well, I'd make the assumption that if Josh didn't have it, then one of us does. As I was the one who was with Jewel of Happiness when she died, I'm the next logical target.'

'If Water Dragon's bully boys start picking us off one by one, it's going to be blatantly obvious something is going on. So, what other option does he have?'

It was a moment or two before I realised what she was getting at. 'He might just send a policeman to lull me into a false sense of security and hand over the key without a fuss.'

She nodded. 'Perhaps you were right to be suspicious. I should have trusted your instincts.'

Any feeling of self-congratulation I might have had at not falling for the false Detective Inspector Sakamoto's ploy dissipated quickly. I may have jumped one hurdle, but realistically, Water Dragon was not about to stop anytime soon.

I felt for the small bunch of keys in my trouser pocket and pulled it out, keeping it below the level of the table. Even so, I took a quick glance around to check no one was looking our way.

'Who'd have thought one tiny key could cause such mayhem.' I shook my head.

Although I had no immediate need of the key to the front door to my aunt's flat or my luggage key; after Josh's room had been ransacked, I'd decided they were no safer locked in my room safe than in my pocket.

Aunt Jessica looked down at them. 'Which is which?

'The one with the square head is for the padlock for my grip, and this is the one Jewel of Happiness slipped in my shirt pocket.'

'They're actually quite different, aren't they?' She peered a little closer. It's not just the head that's circular, the barrel is round not flat like your padlock key.'

'Here. You take it.' Impulsively, I wrestled the key from the fob and held it out to Aunt Jessica.

Her eyebrows shot up and she stared at me for a second or two.

'Take it,' I urged again.

'But why?'

'I just feel it will be safer with you.'

I couldn't explain why I felt that way, but I knew it was the right thing to do.

CHAPTER 30

Our hotel in Tokyo was within walking distance of the railway station. In complete contrast to the one we had just left, the facade of the Tokyo Excel Hotel was a soulless white wall punctured by ten rows of windows that stretched for 100 yards along the busy inner-city street.

Gerri checked in while the rest of us found ourselves a place to perch on the padded benches beyond the reception desk to sip our welcome drinks.

'Do you want to sit down? We can bunch up a bit more,' Isabel said looking up at me.

'I'm fine. Though I will just plonk these things here if you don't mind keeping an eye on them for a couple of minutes. The laptop and all the camera gear are a bit heavy.' I eased all the straps off my shoulders and stacked everything on the floor by the end of the bench.

Isabel took a sip of the pale liquid in the small ceramic bowl and pulled a face before looking round for somewhere to put it.

'Here, shall I take it?'

'Thank you.' She gave me a beaming smile and I took both bowls – mine as well as hers – and made my way over to the tray on one of the stands.

Joanna stood there, a blank look on her face.

'Seems like we've both been abandoned,' I joked, with a nod at Aunt Jessica and Lucy laughing together on one of the couches.

'Hmm. They do seem to be thick as thieves, don't they? They always seem to be together these days.' I'd obviously struck a nerve. Joanna was clearly feeling left out.

'Have you tried taking a dip in any of the onsens yet? There're supposed to be several large ones in this hotel,' I said in an attempt to change the subject. 'After what Gerri said about them being fed by the hot springs at the last place, I meant to give it a try, but somehow I never got round to it. We didn't seem to be there that long.'

She managed a smile. 'You missed a treat. There's been one in nearly all the hotels we've stayed in, but the one yesterday afternoon was by far the best. As we're all free for what's left of the rest of the afternoon, I think I might just check out one here, assuming Lucy is up for it, before we go and find somewhere to eat.'

Gerri was back with the keys. I'd managed to put a smile back on Joanna's face. That's my good deed for the day, I thought to myself as I went to pick up my stuff.

Our main suitcases that had been driven from Nagoya were waiting outside our rooms.

'That's a relief,' I said to Aunt Jessica. 'Not that I thought they'd go missing, but it's nice not to have to wait around for them. You go in and I'll bring your case in for you.'

I pulled up the handle and dragged it behind me. The short corridor past the bathroom was only a couple of inches wider than the door.

'Talk about going from the sublime to the ridiculous!' I dropped the laptop and briefcase onto the bed and surveyed the room.

'It is a bit cramped in here, isn't it?'

Aunt Jessica had squeezed between the side of the bed and the wardrobe to give me room, but now I was trapped as the case occupied the space between the end of the bed and the drawers.

'With thirteen and a half million people all crammed into one city, what else can you expect?' She pulled the stuff dumped at the foot of the bed out of the way to make some space. 'Here, lift it onto the bed.'

'All I can say is, thank goodness we have a room each. This is supposed to be a double room, but one of you would have to sit on the bed and pull your feet up if the other person wanted to move around.'

'Stop exaggerating. What do you want to do now?' She glanced at her watch. 'It's far too early to eat, but we could go out and explore the local area.'

'Is that what you fancy doing?'

'Not especially. Have you something else in mind?'

'Actually, after that long journey, I'd rather like a soak in the onsen. While we were waiting for our keys just now, Joanna was telling me how much she enjoyed the one in the previous hotel.'

'Sounds like a good idea. It's just gone half five, how about we meet back up here at seven o'clock.'

'Okeydokey. I'll give you a knock then.'

I picked up my daypack and went to explore my room next door.

It was about five past seven when I knocked on Aunt Jessica's door.

'Sorry I'm a bit late. Are you ready?'

'Just let me switch off my laptop.'

I followed her in and waited while she sat back on the bed and picked up the laptop.

'Did you go for a soak?'

She shook her head. 'I was going to, but I just wanted to look up something on the internet and I got carried away. By the time I'd found what I wanted, it was too late.'

'Oh?'

'Come and take a look.'

She shifted across and I crawled onto the bed beside her.

'It's obvious our Water Dragon must be a pretty powerful guy if he can get his minions to follow us all over Hokkaido. I've been trying to find out who calls the shots. I didn't really expect to come up with anything concrete, but I've found a few possibilities.' She picked up her writing pad and I could see straight away the top page was covered in her florid scrawl. 'I tried looking up the ten richest men in Japan. It took quite a bit of lateral thinking, but looking at the histories, I've whittled it down to these five. Although I could find nothing that specifically linked any of their names with any of the investigations carried out by Mio Kimura, which, if you remember, is White Tiger's real name, it seems that questions have been asked about aspects of the subsidiary businesses in their empires. But that's not actually the interesting bit. I thought I'd look through the newspaper headlines for the week or so before we arrived. There was one big story.'

She clicked onto one of the tabs and opened a page on an international news agency site
showing an article with the headline, "Murder of Bank President Rocks Japanese Finance Markets".

I scanned the first couple of paragraphs of dense print, but it went on for pages. 'Okay, just give me the gist.'

'The president of one of the major Japanese banks was found in his office with his throat cut. The interesting thing is that he wasn't supposed to be in Kyoto at all. All the staff thought he was in Tokyo. Although nothing had ever been proved, the bank had come under suspicion for laundering money.'

'You think Water Dragon was eliminating a rival?'

She shook her head. 'That's not the interesting bit. I tried to find out if there was any connection between this man and White Tiger. Do you remember that article we found in the days after her death that suggested that she was about to expose one of Japan's leading yakuza bosses? The article hinted that someone within this man's outfit was about to hand over irrefutable evidence.'

'I remember reading it, but I forget the detail.'

'I've been looking at it again. And either it's a mighty big set of coincidences or everything slots into place. The fact that he was in Kyoto incognito, plus the suggestion that his bank was being used to launder yakuza money, implies he knew what was going on.'

'You think he was White Tiger's informant?'

'If he knew he was under threat, he could have taken elaborate precautions. What if that key belongs to a box in one of his vaults?'

'It's possible I suppose.'

'It looks like White Tiger wasn't the only one who'd made it her mission to track down and bring to justice these yakuza lords. The journalist who wrote this article is also the one who did the obituary piece on Mio Kimura that we read in Hiroshima. Apparently, this "Voice from the East" as he calls himself, is the leading Far East correspondent for a major international news agency. He's written several pieces about Mio Kimura praising her legal attempts to expose corruption. As a journalist, he can sail a lot closer to the wind than the lawyer. He doesn't pull his punches and the way I read it, the men he's referring to are only quite thinly disguised. Sadly, I don't know enough about these Japanese highfliers to work out who he's getting at.'

Aunt Jessica showed me a couple of the articles and I could see her point.

'If he's right, then the man he's referring to here has been responsible for eliminating a whole string of people who dared to oppose him.'

'Exactly.'

'Could he be our Water Dragon do you think?'

She pulled a face. 'We can't rule it out. Which means we need to tread very carefully indeed.'

I ran my fingers through my hair.

'Seems to me, you have two options; either you…'

'I'm *not* handing over the key to DCI Sakamoto…'

She put up a hand to stop me. 'That wasn't what I was going to suggest. Either we put you on the next available flight back to Heathrow, or we come up with a really good plan.'

'I may not be Superman, but I couldn't live with myself if I turned my back on the whole thing. I know it's not logical, but I feel responsible for the deaths of both Jewel of Happiness and White Tiger. If I hadn't hesitated those few seconds when I heard her cry out, I might have got there in time to stop that assassin cutting her throat. Same with White Tiger. If I'd not dithered about and made more effort to give her the key when I first saw her, she wouldn't have been wandering about in the gardens trying to find me.'

'But the man would have tracked her down anyway and Water Dragon would have the key. All the evidence against him would have been lost forever. There's no point in ifs and maybes, so stop feeling guilty. We need to concentrate on finding someone here in Japan to give the key to who can uncover the evidence and finish the job that Jewel of Happiness and White Tiger set out to do.'

'And how in the name of all that's holy do we do that?'

'I haven't the remotest idea.'

CHAPTER 31

Our morning tour next day began with the Tokyo Tower – good views from the top, but nothing special – followed by a visit to yet another shrine. Both places were crowded, but I noticed that Aunt Jessica took great care to ensure that we were always in the centre of our small group. She even had her arm tucked into mine for much of the time. She didn't say it, but it was clear that she had no intention of letting me out of her sight.

The next stop on our itinerary was a walk to Hama Rikyu Garden, which according to our local guide – an elderly gentleman named Tsubasa – was created in 1654 and was once the private residence of the Tokugawa Shogun. Once he'd finished his spiel, we were free to wander round the extensive gardens at leisure.

There were far fewer people around and, dragging me with her, Aunt Jessica quickened her pace to catch up with the two Parkes sisters and straightaway struck up a conversation. Although Aunt Jessica appeared to have developed something of a bond with Lucy, I'd never felt at ease with the woman since that first time I'd met her in the hotel lift when she'd caught me looking down at her cleavage and I'd made some crass remark.

Before long, Joanna and I were strolling in front of the other two as they chatted away nineteen to the dozen.

'Did you try out the onsen yesterday?' I asked desperately trying to find something to say.

'Uh-huh. How about you?'

'I did too.' I glanced back at Aunt Jessica and Lucy, but they were too busy talking to pay any attention to me. I took the opportunity to see if anyone was following us or showing us any undue attention, but apart from a few of our party some distance behind, there was no one within a hundred yards of us.

I became aware that Joanna had said something to me.

'Sorry, I missed that. What did you say?'

She gave me a bright smile. 'Nothing important, only that it seems strange that we'll be heading home the day after tomorrow. These last few days have gone with a rush.'

Two days! That's all the time I had left to come up with a plan. 'Hmm. It's strange how the first half of a holiday seem to stretch out, but as soon as you get halfway through, the days flash past.'

'Exactly.'

After that, conversation got a little easier and for a short while, I forgot about any possible followers.

We reached a junction and I was about to take the left fork when I felt a hand on my arm.

'Oops. Sorry, Lucy.' She'd made me jump when I'd felt her touch and we bumped into each other as I'd turned too quickly to see what was happening.

'No problem. Let's go that way. See that sweet little bridge over there?'

We changed direction and as I turned back, I caught sight of a movement further along the left path. Someone had just moved back behind the tree. It was probably perfectly innocent, but in my over-sensitive state, I was ready to suspect everything that seemed out of kilter. If it hadn't been for Lucy, I might have led us all past a stalker or even a potential ambush. Common sense quickly dispelled that thought. I was jumping at shadows. Nonetheless, it took a good minute for my heart rate to return to normal.

Over lunch, I casually asked Aunt Jessica, 'Did you spot

anyone tailing us this morning?'

She looked up sharply, her soup spoon halfway to her lips. 'Did you?'

'I thought I saw someone quickly duck behind a tree when I looked in his direction, but it was probably my over-active imagination.'

'I expect so.' She went back to her miso soup, though I noted that she hadn't actually answered my question.

I finished my noodles, pushed the empty plate to one side and took the city map and couple of tourist leaflets I'd picked up in the hotel lobby from my pocket. 'What would you like to do this afternoon?'

'Let's have a look at the map.'

I opened it out and laid it on the table between us.

'We're not that far from the Imperial Palace. If we take this road and along here,' I traced the route with my finger, 'We should get a good view of it from this side of the water.'

'I'm pretty sure that's on our itinerary for tomorrow.'

Neither of us had thought to bring a copy so we looked through the various leaflets for some ideas. There were several parks and gardens all resplendent with the last flowering of the cherry blossom, but though neither of us put it into words, we instinctively wanted to ensure that wherever we chose, we needed to be surrounded by people and not exposed on our own.

'All the others seem to have opted to go shopping,' I said tentatively.

She pulled a face. 'A waste of a free afternoon if you ask me. How about a museum? There's a flyer here for the Edo-Tokyo Museum. Say's here it's got a life-size replica of the Nihonbashi bridge leading into Edo; the Nakamuraza theatre; and scale models of towns and buildings from the Edo, Meiji and Shōwa periods. What do you think?'

'I'm happy with that. If you don't mind keeping an eye on the camera equipment, I'll nip to the gents. You can work out how we get there while you're waiting.'

'No problem.'

'Back in a tick.' I left her studying the metro map.

The men's room was empty when I went in. I still hadn't quite got used to the soft music of mountain streams tumbling downhill, leaves gently blowing in the wind and melodic birdsong that appear to be played in nearly all the public toilets in Japan. Even the noise of the hand drier seemed more muted than back home.

As I went to leave, the door pushed open and a man came in. I stepped to the right and he to his left and we did that unintentional dance that people do when they try and pass each other. I heard someone coming out of one of the cubicles behind me and suddenly I felt a sharp prick like a wasp sting in my upper arm. Clutching at my arm with my other hand, I turned to see behind me, but I obviously spun too quickly because my head began to spin. My vision blurred, my knees gave way and I felt decidedly woozy.

I dimly remember each of the men taking hold of my arms and guiding me out into the corridor. My brain was too foggy to resist or even protest. They propelled me along to a door that led outside to where a large black car was waiting. A third man was standing with the rear door open. The last thing I remember was being bundled into the back of the car.

CHAPTER 32

The room was dark when I came to and it took several moments to get my bearings and remember what had happened. I was sitting in an upright chair, my arms pulled tight behind with my wrists clamped together. It was probably the cramp in my shoulders that had roused me to consciousness. I arched my back and managed wiggle them a fraction but not enough to ease the pain. My legs had been tightly bound with gaffer tape from calf to ankle to the two front legs of the chair.

The air smelt stale and dusty. I had no way of knowing how long I'd been unconscious. Apart from a low distant rumble that might have been traffic or perhaps some machinery in the far reaches of the building, the place was silent.

Slowly, my eyes adjusted to the gloom and I took stock of my surroundings. There were no windows in the cavernous room which appeared to be in an empty warehouse. I could see nothing but bare walls and an uncluttered floor. Apart from the chair I was strapped to and a small table a few feet to my right, there was no other furniture. On the table lay my jacket and something white – my handkerchief and presumably the rest of the contents of my pockets. Difficult to tell in the virtual dark.

Some light filtered through from behind me. I tried to turn my head to see where it was coming from, but it was too far back, and the movement made my head spin and the dull ache at my temples increased to a painful throb. I thought of trying to hitch the whole chair round, but the way my ankles were strapped with only the tips of my toes reaching the floor meant I couldn't get any real purchase with my feet.

Whether it was because of the cold or my rising fear, I found myself shivering uncontrollably. This was no time to panic, I told myself sharply.

For the next ten minutes, I tried to free my hands, twisting the tape that tied my wrists. I tried to get the little finger of my bottom hand under the tape but all I succeeded in doing was cutting into my skin with my nail.

I shouted for help and the sound of unhurried footsteps came from behind me – at least two people as far as I could tell. The door scraped the floor as it was pushed open. I called out again, but the only answer was a low mutter. Definitely not my rescuers.

One of them must have flicked a light switch. After the dark of the past half hour, the intense bright light almost blinded me. I rocked back in the chair and had to throw myself forwards to stop the chair toppling backwards.

A coarse laugh came from behind me and though he spoke in Japanese, it wasn't difficult to interpret he was making some joke at my expense.

'What do you want? Why am I here?'

My questions went unanswered.

I'm not sure what was worse – being left alone in the dark or having the two goons behind me completely ignoring my presence. If I was going to be interrogated, it was obviously not going to be by either of these two.

A third man, dressed in a smart business suit, arrived not long after. He marched forward and stood in front of me, staring intensely as though inspecting me for purchase. I stared back. I wasn't going to give him the satisfaction of showing the fear I felt. His wasn't a face I recognised.

He turned to one of the others who had followed in his wake and said something I took to be a question. Him I did recognise. The man who had come into the toilet. I had never seen the man who had come up behind me, but I assumed the second man had been my other captor – the one who'd stuck the syringe in my arm.

All three men were now over at the table and looking through the contents of my pockets. Looking rather pleased with himself, Syringe Man picked up my key ring and handed it to Mr Business Suit. All he got in return was a sharp retort at which his face fell, and he dropped his head like some naughty schoolboy.

Mr Business Suit seized the keys and marched over to me, dangled the small bunch by my luggage key and snapped in heavily accented English, 'What does this open?'

'It's the key to the padlock for my grip.'

'Grip? What is grip?'

'My holdall, luggage bag.'

He slung the keys back onto the table barely missing one of the men.

'Where is other key?'

'What key?'

'The key Geisha give you.'

I shook my head. 'I don't understand. Nobody gave me a key.'

Strictly speaking she hadn't. Not actually hand it over to me. She'd slipped it in my pocket without me ever realising.

How long I could keep this up I didn't know. These men were killers. Did I stand a better chance pleading ignorance or telling them what they wanted? It was a gamble either way. The only thing that stopped me revealing the key's whereabouts was knowing I'd be putting Aunt Jessica in danger. That I was not prepared to do.

All three men went into a huddle.

Eventually, Mr Business Suit pulled out a mobile and punched in a number. The conversation he had with whoever it was at the other end was brief. At the end of the call, all three walked to the door.

'Leave the light on,' I shouted.

The light snapped off, the door slammed shut and the darkness was absolute.

It looked as though there would be a wait before the next man in this corruption food chain arrived. So Mr. Business Suit, whoever he was, was not Water Dragon.

The only bright spot was that I was still alive. But for how long?

CHAPTER 33

What seemed like hours went by. So long I was beginning to wonder if I'd been abandoned. Would my desiccated body ever be found? I knew the human body can survive for several weeks without food but for how long without water? A week maybe, ten days? I'd go mad long before that.

I'd managed to wriggle my arms high enough to ease the cramp in my shoulders, but my lower legs had been so tightly strapped that the lack of circulation gave me pins and needles. Only by constantly flexing and unflexing my feet could I get any kind of relief, but every time I stopped the painful tingle came back after only a few minutes. I knew that I ought to be working out what to do next, come up with some sort of escape plan, but I had no notion of how to go about it. The knowledge that Aunt Jessica would now be summoning help from every conceivable quarter was some consolation. I tried not to consider how she could have the remotest idea of where I was being held. Not even I had a clue.

The sound of a distant siren gradually increased. I tried not to get my hopes up. There was no knowing if it was even a police car. Minutes later I heard a vehicle drawing up on the other side of the wall. The siren was switched off and a car door slammed. Only one car, so no rescue squad. I listened intently but I couldn't hear footsteps nor was there any sound from the opening of an outside door.

It seemed an age before the sound of swift footsteps

came along the corridor. The door opened and once again the light was snapped on. I turned my head as far as I could to watch the newcomer's approach.

'Chief Inspector Sakamoto.' I could tell by the angry expression on the man's face, he was not here to set me free anytime soon. I'd been about to make some sarcastic remark about Japanese honour and appointing a corrupt policeman to take charge of investigating corruption in high places, but quickly thought better of it. My situation was bad enough without making things worse. My only hope was to delay things for as long as possible in the remote hope that Aunt Jessica would somehow manage to mount a rescue.

'Stop playing games, Mr Hamilton-James. Tell me the whereabouts of the key.'

I shook my head. 'As I've already told your colleague here,' I nodded at Mr Business Suit who appeared by my chair. 'I know nothing about any key.'

The inspector gave a derisive snort and signalled to someone behind me. Syringe Man padded forward, a pair of pliers in his hand.

'Last chance, Mr Hamilton-James. Either you tell me where you have put the safe box key or Hamaguchi will take great delight in pulling out your fingernails. One. By. One.'

Syringe Man gave me an evil grin that spread from ear to ear.

How I managed to stop my bladder from letting go, I have no idea. Didn't want to show the bastard just how terrified I really was, I suppose.

My mouth had gone dry, but I managed to croak. 'Please, I keep telling you, I don't have any key. I have no idea where it is. Why won't you believe me?'

The tape binding my hands was cut and my arms fell to my sides. I slid my hands onto my thighs and gently flexed my wrists to ease stiffness trying not to cry out as blood rushed back into my fingers.

Syringe man took a step towards me and I clamped my arms across my chest balling my fists under my armpits.

'No! I can't tell you what I don't know.' My voice rose to a scream.

As the man took another step towards me, I swung my body away from him, the chair toppled over with a crash. My head banged on the concrete floor. Everything went black.

I was only dimly aware of the commotion around me when I came to. I opened my eyes but shut them promptly when the bright light seared my eyeballs. Strong arms held on to me as my chair was gently lifted upright. The movement made me feel vaguely sick. My head was throbbing, an intense pain shot through my left elbow and blood dripped from a bad graze stretching from my left elbow to my palm.

He spoke to me softly, but the words didn't make any sense. I just wanted to lie down and go to sleep.

Someone must have freed my legs but when the rest of the tape was pulled from my bare wrist, the sudden pain jerked me back to full consciousness.

'Sorry about that,' said the kindly voice of the man still kneeling at my feet.

He took my right wrist, looking at his watch. It was then that I noticed the stethoscope round his neck. When he'd finished, he nodded to the man behind my chair who been supporting me, and I was gently lifted onto a stretcher trolley.

'Ow! My shoulder.'

When I next opened my eyes, I saw Aunt Jessica sitting in a chair by my bedside.

'Hi,' I managed to croak.

She gave me a radiant smile and said softly, 'You're awake. About time too. You've been out for hours.'

'What time is it?'

She looked at her watch. 'Almost two o'clock.'

'In the morning?' I said incredulously. Could it really be twelve hours since I'd been abducted from the restaurant?

She nodded.

Before I had time to say anything more, a nurse came to check me over. There was a drip in my arm and the hum of hospital machinery all around me. I looked round the room. There were three other beds, but they were empty. I had the ward to myself.

The nurse took my temperature, checked my heart rate and blood pressure, wrote up the results on my chart, then turned not to me but Aunt Jessica. 'Everything appear okay. Doctor come soon.'

Once she'd left, I tried to haul myself into a sitting position.

'Take it easy, sweetie. You've been through the wars.' She put an arm under my shoulders, lifted me high enough to wedge a pillow behind me and laid me back again into a semi upright position.

'How did you manage to find me?'

'Later. Right now, the police want to speak to you.'

I frowned. 'How do you know they are the good guys? Our Chief Inspector Sakamoto certainly wasn't.'

There was a knock, but it was Lucy who put her head round the door not the police.

'How's the patient?'

'Fine,' I mumbled.

'You don't look it, I must say,' she said with a cheeky grin.

Without invitation, she pulled a chair from the side wall, brought it over to the bed and sat down.

'I think the police are waiting to interview me.' I tried not to sound haughty.

'They're out there now. While they're conferring, I thought I'd pop in and see how you are.' The woman had an infernal cheek. What was she even doing in the hospital let alone in the middle of the night?

'It's thanks to Lucy, we managed to find you at all,' my aunt said. 'When you didn't come back into the restaurant, I wasn't sure what to do. Contacting the police was no guarantee so I rang Gerri and told her you were missing, and that I was on my way to the embassy. It took some time to get someone to believe my story, by which time Lucy had arrived.'

'I don't understand.'

Lucy took up the story. 'Your room had been ransacked like Josh's. When they couldn't find the key on you, they obviously tore your room apart looking for it.'

'You know about the key?'

Lucy smiled, but it was Aunt Jessica who answered. 'Meet the real Fox.'

'You?'

Lucy nodded.

At that point the door opened, and two men came in, one in uniform and the other plain clothes. Aunt Jessica and Lucy got to their feet.

It was Lucy who introduced them. 'This is Peter Harris from the British Embassy and he will vouch for Superintendent Ito from the Organized Crime Department of the Criminal Affairs Bureau, part of Interpol. We'll leave you to it.'

'Is that the same lot as Chief Inspector Sakamoto's mob?' I asked, once the two women had gone, unable to keep the scepticism from my voice.

Superintendent Ito smiled. 'No. The Special Investigation Department is a different section altogether. If it's any consolation, Sakamoto and his associates are now in custody. We have had an eye on him for some time. Neither he nor his associates are talking so far, which means we still haven't got any hard evidence against the man who we believe is at the head of this whole network. Not that we expected to. They know what will happen to their families if they do. That is really why I would like to ask you a few questions now, if you feel up to it.'

I nodded. 'I'm not sure I can help.'

'I already have a full statement from Miss Hamilton so all I need from you is an account of what happened from the time you were taken from the restaurant until you were

202

rescued.'

It didn't take long to give my statement. My captors hadn't mentioned any other names so I could give them nothing to help in their investigation.

'That is all for now, Mr Hamilton-James. We will let you get some rest.'

'What will happened to Chief Inspector Sakamoto? Do you have any evidence to charge him with?'

Superintendent Ito smiled. 'Oh yes. He and his partners were still in the warehouse when we arrived. They will not be able to wriggle out of that one. They have already been charged with kidnap and once the word gets round that Sakamoto is in custody, it will not be long before we find people who will provide evidence of his intimidation and extortion tactics. By the time we have finished, not only will he be spending a long time behind bars, he will never be in a position to go back to his old ways.'

Once the two men had gone, the initial relief I'd felt knowing that Sakamoto was no longer a threat was overshadowed by nagging doubt. Was I really safe? Water Dragon obviously had far reaching tentacles. Just because one had been chopped off, didn't guarantee I was finally out of danger.

The nurse came in to check me over again and remove my drip. 'All good.'

'In that case, can I go back to my hotel?'

'No, no,' she protested. 'You have concussion from fall. Doctor need check you over in morning.'

She fluffed up my pillows and settled me down for what was left of the night, then turned down the lights.

'You need something, you press call button.'

As if I could sleep. There were far too many questions buzzing round my head. How had Lucy known where to find me? If she was Fox, what part did Josh have to play in all this? Where was the key now, and not least, what did the dammed thing open?

CHAPTER 34

Whether it was because of some medication I'd been given or pure exhaustion, I must have dropped off quite quickly. I opened my eyes to see a figure standing by the bed.

'How are you feeling?'

This nurse was young and pretty and, unlike the solemn night nurse, gave me a warm smile as she proceeded to take my temperature, pulse and blood pressure.

'All normal. Let me take a look at your dressing.'

She eased away the tape that held the gauze covering on my arm and inspected the graze. 'The bleeding has stopped, and it looks clean.'

'Your English is very good. Have you been to America?'

'My sister lives in California and my parents and I have visited several times.'

She straightened my covers.

'The police returned your coat and the rest of your things.' She made a sweeping gesture to cover my jacket hanging over the back of a chair and my mobile, money and handkerchief on the bedside table.

'Where are the rest of my clothes?'

Lying there in a hospital gown, I felt ridiculously exposed.

'I'll go and check, but I believe they had to be cut off you when you arrived. The breakfast trolley will be along soon, but if you need anything.'

'I'll press the call button.'

She smiled and shut the door.

Aunt Jessica arrived a couple of hours later.

'You look ten times better than last night.'

'Apart from a very tender shoulder and a sore elbow, I'm fighting fit. Well, ready to leave here, anyway. As soon as the doctor's done his rounds and given his say so, I can leave.'

'Great. I've brought you a set of clean clothes. I'm afraid a great deal of your stuff was ripped up when your room was searched, but I managed to find you these. The shirt's a bit crumpled but it was the best I could find.'

'I have a hundred questions to ask.'

'First of all, I want a blow-by-blow account of what happened to you from when you left me in the café.'

When Aunt Jessica wants something – she gets. There was no point in arguing so I did as I was told.

'If they didn't hit you, what happened to your arm?' She pointed to the dressing.

'I must have tried to break my fall with it when the chair toppled over. I slid along the floor and it was covered in grit.' I lifted my hand and let out an involuntary groan.

'What's wrong?'

'My shoulder's giving me jip if I forget and move it. It must have taken most of the impact. Luckily it wasn't dislocated or broken, just badly bruised, but you'll have to carry your laptop and camera gear going back. I won't be putting any weight on it anytime soon. Anyway, as I was saying, I must have been knocked unconscious because I've no idea what happened next. When they left, I just can't say.'

'Sounds like the police arrived just in time.'

I shuddered at the thought of what Chief Inspector Sakamoto might have done to me as I lay on the floor.

'Did I hear you say last night that it was Lucy who found me? How did she know where I was?'

She shrugged her shoulders. 'No idea. That you'll have to ask her.'

'But I don't understand…'

'Let me tell you what I do know. When you didn't come

back, I asked the waiter if he'd check the men's toilets for me. No one had seen you leave, and I knew you wouldn't just walk out. I rang your mobile, but it had been switched off. Then I knew for sure you'd been abducted.'

'They must have switched it off. I certainly didn't.'

When the two of us are out together, we always leave our phones on in case we get separated.

'I didn't want to go to the police after what you'd said about Chief Inspector Sakamoto, so I decided to go to the British Embassy. The first response of the man I spoke to was to ask me if I'd rung your mobile and if I'd checked the hotel to see if you'd returned there without me. He got short shrift from me; I can tell you. Then he asked if I'd reported your disappearance to the police. I decided trying to explain about police corruption to a desk clerk would only make me sound like some mad old woman, so I mumbled something about knowing that police didn't start looking for missing persons in the first twenty-four hours. He tried to fob me off, but I refused to leave until I'd spoken to someone more senior. It took a while but, in the end he agreed.'

I tried to hide my smile. It didn't take much to picture the scene. I could almost feel sorry for the poor man. Though Aunt Jessica is usually one of the most tolerant and easy-going people I know, it doesn't pay to cross her. She doesn't lose her temper or start shouting; she has the Hamilton women's ability to chop you off at the knees with a look and a well-chosen phrase or two.

'It took forever but eventually I was shown into an office. After I'd explained everything that had happened to Josh, he wrote down the details, but I wasn't convinced he believed me or that he would take any action. He took my mobile number and told me to go back to the hotel and wait for a call.'

No doubt leaving him with a few choice words about what she might do if he didn't get back to her in the very near future, I thought.

'It was gone four o'clock by the time I got back to the

hotel. Gerri was waiting for me and we went up to my room together. That's when I noticed your door wasn't closed properly. I went in and the room was a total mess.'

'Like Josh's?'

'Exactly. I got back to the Embassy straight away. I'd insisted on the chap I'd spoken to giving me his card, so I went straight to him. Give him his due, he did pull out all the stops then.'

'But how did they know where I'd been taken?'

'Well that bit I'm not sure about. All I know is that Lucy arrived as all this kerfuffle was going on and she sort of took over.'

'I don't understand.'

'I told you she is the real Fox.' Aunt Jessica gave a broad smile and said triumphantly. 'She is also "Voice from the East". Which is why of course she has so many contacts.'

'The reporter who wrote all those articles?'

'Exactly. I've suspected for several days that Lucy must know something. That's why I've been spending so much time with her. Then I realised that it wasn't just me trying to pump her, she was doing exactly the same to me.'

'So that's why she was trying to cosy up to me on that day in Nara.'

'Exactly. She'd guessed you had to have the key.'

'And when that didn't work, she befriended you knowing I'd tell you everything. But why then did she make a play for Josh?'

She gave a slight shake of the head. 'No idea. Hedging her bets, maybe? We'll have to ask her when we get back.'

It was another hour before the doctor came and I was officially discharged. Getting dressed was tricky. Aunt Jessica had to help ease my arm into my shirt as I couldn't lift it without sending shooting pains across my shoulder and the whole of my left side.

I decided not to even try putting my arm into the sleeve of my jacket, draping it over my shoulder.

'Would it help if we used my scarf as a sling? If nothing else, it will remind you not to aggravate your shoulder by constantly moving your arm.'

It felt as though I was milking the situation in a plea for sympathy, but I have to admit, it made me a great deal more comfortable.

'Could you pass me my phone and the rest of my stuff, please.'

She slipped the mobile into my trouser pocket along with my handkerchief and picked up my watch. 'There's a scratch at the back here. Looks as though they even took the back off your watch.'

I frowned. 'They obviously weren't sure what they were looking for. The key may be small but not that tiny. Have you still got it?'

She shook her head. 'I gave it to Lucy.'

'Do you think that's wise? You only have her word for it that she is who she says she is.'

'No. She has contacts over here including that nice Mr Harris from the British Embassy. That's how she got the authorities to swing in to action. Besides after I'd given it to her, the two of them, plus Superintendent Ito went to Kenji Nakamura's bank to retrieve the evidence he'd hidden to convict Water Dragon.'

There were a great many questions I wanted to ask Lucy Parkes when I met up with her again.

'Come on, let's get going.' She turned back to the bedside table and began to scoop up my loose change.

'What's this?' She held up a plain bronze disc the size and colour of a one-yen coin.

'No idea. Perhaps I was given it as change when I bought something. All of seven pence, so hardly an issue.'

'Okay. If that's it, let's go and find a taxi and get you back to the hotel.'

'Actually,' I hesitated. 'Do you mind if we went to get something to eat first? I haven't had anything for nearly twenty-four hours. Hospital breakfasts don't really cater for western palates and I'm starving.'

She laughed. 'Not sure I can find you anywhere that does bacon and eggs, but let's go and explore.'

CHAPTER 35

Aunt Jessica and I had a long, leisurely lunch and I was feeling much more my old self by the time the taxi pulled up outside our hotel shorty after three o'clock.

'I expect everyone else will still be out on the tour.'

'That's good. To be honest, I don't feel up to everyone demanding to know what happened. They're bound to want all the gory details.'

'Hmm. I think we ought to come up with a cover story. I believe Gerri has told them all that you ended up in hospital because of a fall. The last thing she and the travel company want is passengers getting a hint of anything that might get into the media and put off potential customers.'

'Makes sense. People being murdered and abducted by corrupt Japanese oligarchs won't exactly encourage future bookings.'

'Precisely.'

'Good to see you back, Mr Hamilton-James,' the softly spoken receptionist said as I passed the front desk.

'That's Kimi,' Aunt Jessica said as we waited for the lift. 'She was so helpful yesterday. I think I might get a small present for her as a thank you. But first let's get you settled.'

We went straight to my room. 'Key card?'

I shook my head. 'It's gone. It was in the inside pocket of my anorak. They must have taken it when I was kidnapped.'

'That explains how your captors got in of course.'

'Won't it be a scene of crime or whatever they call it over

here? And I don't suppose there's been time to clean it up since it was ransacked either.'

'No problem. The police released the room first thing this morning and, thanks to Japanese efficiency, the maids were already in the process of clearing up when I went to get some clean clothes to bring you in hospital.'

She opened her door and we both went in.

'You wait there while I pop down to reception and get them to programme another key card for you.'

I lay down on her bed staring up at the ceiling and closed my eyes.

I must have fallen asleep almost at once because the curtains had been half drawn when I woke. Using my right elbow so as not to aggravate my shoulder, I gingerly pushed myself upright and a piece of paper fluttered from my chest.

"Sweetie – didn't have the heart to wake you so I've just popped out to the shops to get some presents to take home. Won't be long, love J."

Aunt Jessica bustled in ten minutes later, dumping two carrier bags of shopping on the end of the bed.

'What on earth is that lot for?'

'Presents for my sisters. One from each of us. I didn't think you'd want to face the shops and we'll be off to the airport first thing. I got this for your mother from you.' She gently eased a well-wrapped package from one of the bags and proceeded to free the contents from the layers of paper and bubble-wrap. 'Do you think she'll like it?'

She handed me a tall delicately shaped vase painted with a stylised elongated picture of a woman in traditional kimono and obi with hair piled high like a geisha.

'She'll love it. I only hope I can get it back in one piece.'

We spent the next ten minutes exploring the various presents she'd bought. Not only does Aunt Jessica have great taste, she has an uncanny knack for finding just the right thing that would appeal to my two difficult aunts, Maud and Edwina. It's something I never seem able to do. They would probably guess that Aunt Jessica had had a hand in the choosing, but what the hell – it certainly wasn't something I was about to lose sleep over.

We were interrupted by a knock at the door.

'I expect that's Gerri. They are probably back from the afternoon tour by now. I texted her earlier to say you were fine and back in the hotel.'

As it turned out, it was Lucy who followed Aunt Jessica into the main body of the room. The flighty, girly persona had gone. With her hair pulled back in a severe chignon, she looked every inch the no-nonsense hard-headed journalist.

'I thought you might like to know that Water Dragon has been arrested and taken into custody and a massive round up of all his associates is now going on. You can relax.'

'That's a relief,' said Aunt Jessica.

Lucy turned to me with a smile. 'How's the patient?'

I gave her a weak grin. 'Aunt Jessica said it was you I had to thank for my rescue.'

'Think nothing of it.'

'But how did you know where I was?'

'Ahh. That's another reason I popped in. Can I have my tracker back? Replacements don't come cheap. I hope your captors didn't find it or you've chucked it.'

The penny dropped. 'The bronze disc. But when did you put it in my pocket?'

She gave me a mischievous grin. 'When we were walking in the park. I was hoping to tag along with you both for the rest of the day, but when I saw we'd picked up a shadow, I couldn't be sure if he was after you or if my cover had been blown. I decided it was best to separate and see what happened, but I couldn't leave you totally exposed.'

I remembered how she had bumped into me when she'd insisted on taking the right fork in the path. I fished in my pocket and found her tracker.

'I thought you were a journalist not a spy,' I joked. 'But I still don't understand what this whole business is about.'

'Perhaps it's best if I explain the whole thing from the

beginning.' We moved all the presents aside and Aunt Jessica and I settled ourselves at the head of the double bed facing Lucy perched at the foot. 'Do you remember a woman was murdered when we were at the shrine at Hiroshima?'

'White Tiger. The lawyer trying to bring those responsible for corruption on a massive scale to justice,' I interrupted.

Lucy smiled. 'Exactly. I see you two have done your homework.'

'Does this have anything to do with the banker who was murdered in Kyoto just before we arrived? Aunt Jessica said something about the key opening a safety deposit box kept at his bank?'

She nodded. 'Kenji Nakamura. Indeed, it does.'

'So how does he fit into the picture?'

'Water Dragon lives and works in Tokyo, but three years ago he arranged for certain documents to be stored in the vault of the Kyoto branch of Kenji's bank. It's well known that the Nakamura Bank had been laundering Water Dragon's money for years. Kenji himself was semi-retired and left most of the running of the bank to his son, Gin. Gin was a gambler and ended up in serious debt which made him vulnerable. Gin had no option other than to authorise all Water Dragon's transactions. Kenji didn't find out for some years, but by then he was powerless to do anything about it because Water Dragon threatened to reveal Gin's dealing to the world at large. The bank would've been ruined, and the loss of face would've disgraced the family name for ever. However, things came to a head and Kenji decided enough was enough.'

'What changed his mind?'

'Gin was murdered. He was found with his throat cut. Kenji knew who was responsible and he wanted revenge even if it cost him his own life, so he hatched a plan. All of Water Dragon's accounts are handled by the Tokyo branch so when he arranged for a box of documents to be kept in Kyoto, Kenji was suspicious. As is the case with all boxes entrusted to the bank there are only two keys, one held by the owner and a spare which is kept at the bank and accessible only to the manager. Kenji opened the box and realised that the notebook he discovered inside contained detailed records which could be used in evidence against Water Dragon. Knowing that the man had senior figures in his pocket, Kenji realised the only person he could trust to bring Water Dragon to justice was the lawyer Mio Kimura.'

'White Tiger.'

'Exactly. Kenji knew he was being watched and couldn't walk out of the bank with the documents, let alone take them to her. If he was seen to be going to Hiroshima or she to Kyoto, Water Dragon would know straight away and neither of them would reach their destination. He did the only thing he could think of – remove the contents of Water Dragon's box and hide it in another in the vault.'

'Which is presumably where you come into the picture,' said Aunt Jessica.

'Exactly. As I said, Kenji had no idea who he could trust as an intermediary. Mio suggested me because I'd worked with her before. Plus, I can ensure the world gets to hear whenever the Japanese media is silenced. The corruption extends into every area of influential society. However, I'm not exactly unknown in this part of the world and Kenji knew if I turned up at the bank as me, Water Dragon would work out what we were up to. Kenji insisted I come to Japan in disguise, hence Lucy Parkes – a bone fide tourist.'

'We sort of guessed Joanna isn't your sister.'

Lucy shook her head. 'No. She's one of my researchers.'

'But I still don't understand,' I said. 'Why did Jewel of Happiness have the key?'

Lucy gave a long sigh. 'The trouble was that all his elaborate planning had to be changed when Kenji realised he'd been betrayed by one of his own clerks. With Water Dragon's arrival imminent, Kenji didn't have much time to come up with an alternative. It was impossible to bring forward the date I was due in Japan, so Kenji decided his only option was to pass the key to Jewel of Happiness. He had the details of my itinerary and by coincidence, he was a frequent visitor to her in the tea house.'

'Presumably, Water Dragon got wind of what had happened.'

'Exactly. He had Jewel of Happiness followed. She must have noticed she had a tail that evening, so she was late getting to the tea house. I went to meet her when we first got there, but she hadn't arrived, and I couldn't keep pretending I needed to nip out to the loo throughout the meal.'

'If I'd been there just a minute before, I might have saved her.'

Lucy shook her head. 'I doubt it. You would have been dead too. Just be thankful that if you hadn't arrived when you did, he'd have taken the key and both Kenji and Jewel of Happiness would have died for nothing.'

'I suppose so.'

'At first, I thought her assassin had taken the key before he killed her, but it soon became obvious that the group was being followed so I realised someone in our group must have it. You claimed Jewel of Happiness was dying when you found her and, though it was logical that you had the key, because you didn't mention it, I couldn't be sure which side you were on. On the plus side, it was obvious that Water Dragon had no idea who in the party the key had been given to, either.'

'So why all the business with Josh?' asked Aunt Jessica. 'Why did you make a play for him?'

Lucy raised an eyebrow. 'If I'm honest, at first it was simply a means to help my cover, but by the time we reached Hiroshima, I realised something else was going on. It wasn't until he went missing in Takayama that I managed to work out what it was. I suspected he was passing on information about the group to Water Dragon's cronies.'

'That would explain why he kept disappearing, but how on earth did he get involved with them in the first place?'

'They played a similar trick on him to the one they tried

on Harry. He told me the whole story after he ended up in the hospital. He was approached in Hiroshima by a couple of policemen who claimed that they suspected one of our party was involved in the death of the geisha who had been murdered in the tea house in Kyoto. Josh asked who they suspected, but they fobbed him off saying they couldn't divulge that information. They asked if he would keep them informed if any of our lot disappeared or did anything unexpected. I think he was quite flattered at first and enjoyed being involved in an undercover operation. It wouldn't surprise me if he wasn't offered a substantial bribe as well, though he never admitted to that.'

'So why did they beat him up?'

'As time went on, he became increasingly suspicious and told them he wasn't prepared to answer any more of their questions until he'd checked with the British Embassy.'

'Presumably he came clean to the police after he ended up in hospital.'

'He refused point blank. It took a fair amount of persuading on my part to get any of the story out of him at all. I told him to tell the authorities, but he was terrified. He'd been left for dead and was convinced if he spoke to anyone, they would come for him again. When the offer was made to fly him straight home, he jumped at the chance.'

'Who can blame him. But where does it leave things for us?' Despite Lucy's earlier assurances, even with Water Dragon in custody, I didn't give much for my own chances, especially if I was to be called as a witness at his trial.

'The police will require a statement from you, but the important thing is that you and the rest of the group are all safe. There is nothing to stop you flying back to Heathrow tomorrow as planned. There is no need for me to remain incognito anymore either. I'll be staying on to give evidence at his trial. Things will move very quickly from now on.' She glanced at her watch. 'I need to get over to the agency. I have an article to write. I may not see either of you again before your flight.'

She stood up and held out her hand. 'The world will never be free of corruption, but thanks to you two, a great many influential men will spend the rest of their days behind bars. If you hadn't guarded that key so tenaciously, the notebook would have been destroyed and there would have been no hard evidence. Thank you.'

CHAPTER 36

It was a couple of weeks after we'd returned home before Aunt Jessica and I headed north out of London on the M11 towards Norfolk. She had hired a car – a BMW 5 – for the weekend claiming that we would be able to take my mother and the aunts into Norwich for a slap-up meal and possibly a show if there was anything suitable playing at the Theatre Royal, The Playhouse or the Maddermarket. It was great to get behind the wheel of a car again especially an upmarket model. I missed my old Escort, but even if I could afford a new car, it really wasn't practical if I was going to remain living in London.

Traffic is always worse on a Friday and even though we'd decided to leave after lunch, we made slow progress, stopping and starting until we'd crossed over the M25.

'We are agreed that as far as the family are concerned, Japan was wonderful, and the only excitement was seeing the sights?' I said as we waited at the traffic lights heading into Norwich.

'If you're sure you don't want them to know how you exposed a whole string of master criminals and brought them to justice.'

'Hardly that,' I laughed. 'All I did was hold on to a key instead of handing it over as soon as I found it like any sensible person would have done. Besides, can you really see Aunt Maud and Aunt Edwina believing our story anyway?'

'You may be right, but more to the point, if your mother

discovered half of what had happened, she'd never let me have anything to do with you again. She's already convinced I'm the one leading you astray.'

'Which is true of course.' I received a sharp poke in the arm. 'Hey. That's my bad shoulder.'

'Good. You need to learn a bit more respect for your elders and betters.'

Aunt Jessica's choice of presents went down very well though the Japanese sweets we'd bought were regarded with certain amount of suspicion. I'm not sure Aunt Maud or Aunt Edwina even tried the dried seaweed.

We spent most of Friday evening looking at the photographs. I confess I was rather pleased with my efforts and even the aunts seemed impressed.

'And where are you off to next?' Aunt Edwina asked Aunt Jessica.

'Nothing booked for definite yet, but the tour company are keen for me to accompany the next trip to Iran in the autumn.'

My mother turned her head sharply and her eyes widened. 'Is that a good idea?'

Aunt Jessica gave her a reassuring smile. 'It's one of my regular trips. I've done it four times already and I have to say it's one of my favourites – Persian Palaces and Gardens. Persepolis is an amazing place and the architecture is spectacular. Isfahan should be on every traveller's bucket list and Tehran has the richest collection of crown jewels of any country in the world.'

My mother was clearly unconvinced. She looked at me, but I said nothing. Aunt Jessica and I hadn't discussed her next trip and I had no idea if I would be invited.

'Shall I go and put the kettle on?' I said getting to my feet.

'No dear, you're a guest. You sit there.'

'At least let me help,' I protested and followed my mother out to the kitchen.

Much to my surprise, the whole of Saturday went by without Aunt Maud making any inquiries about my future plans. There were no snide comments about my job prospects and, thanks to Aunt Jessica's presence, no questions about how long I intended to stay in her flat.

It wasn't until Sunday morning that the crunch came.

'It's such a shame you can't stay longer. I see so little of you these days.'

'Sorry Mum. I have to get back tonight because I've a lunchtime shift at the restaurant tomorrow.'

'You've managed to find yourself a job then?' Aunt Maud intervened. 'Doing what exactly?'

Restaurant was probably stretching it a bit. Mario's wasn't exactly an haute cuisine establishment, but it served decent food at reasonable prices. 'I'm working as a sous chef.' Technically that was correct, but I was second in command only because there was only one other cook – Mario himself. 'It's only temporary, covering for the usual chap until he recovers from a broken arm. It's mostly shift work, but at least it'll cover my rent and pay for the course I'm doing at college.'

'A catering course?'

'No. It's a graphic design diploma.'

'It will help him expand his computer and website consultancy,' Aunt Jessica chipped in. 'He's taken on a couple of clients already since we got back from Japan.'

She failed to mention that she was one of them. There hadn't been much time to get Curtis's website up and running yet, but he seemed pleased with the proposals I'd sent him. I had high hopes it might lead to him sending more clients my way.

'Well that all went much better than expected,' I said as we drove out of the village. 'Aunt Maud didn't get her claws into me once.'

'She really isn't that bad you know. She may have a sharp

tongue, but she has a good heart.'

'So you keep telling me. But that doesn't stop me quaking at the knees whenever she turns her beady eye on me.'

'I thought after all you've been through, you were beginning to grow a bit more backbone. Not all members of the female sex are out to get you, you know.'

'I'll take a rain check on that one. It's the powerful ones I can't handle. I never know what they're thinking.'

She shook her head in mock exasperation then leant across and patted my hand on the steering wheel. 'And long may that continue, sweetie!'

ABOUT THE AUTHOR

Judith has three passions in life – writing, travel and ancient history. Her novels are the product of those passions. Her Fiona Mason Mysteries are each set on coach tours to different European countries and her history lecturer Aunt Jessica, accompanies travel tours to more exotic parts of the world.

Born and brought up in Norwich, she now lives with her husband in Wiltshire. Though she wrote her first novel (now languishing in the back of a drawer somewhere) when her two children were toddlers. There was little time for writing when she returned to work teaching Geography in a large comprehensive. It was only after retiring from her headship, that she was able to take up writing again in earnest.

Life is still busy. She spends her mornings teaching Tai Chi and yoga or at line dancing, Pilates and Zumba classes. That's when she's not at sea as a cruise lecturer giving talks on ancient history, writing and writers or running writing workshops.

***

Find out more about Judith at www.judithcranswick.co.uk